Johannes Tinctoris, John Bishop, James A. Hamilton

Hamilton's Celebrated Dictionary

comprising an explanation of 3,500 Italian, French, German, English, and other

musical terms, phrases and abbreviations, also a copious list of musical characters

Johannes Tinctoris, John Bishop, James A. Hamilton

Hamilton's Celebrated Dictionary
comprising an explanation of 3,500 Italian, French, German, English, and other musical terms, phrases and abbreviations, also a copious list of musical characters

ISBN/EAN: 9783337238476

Printed in Europe, USA, Canada, Australia, Japan

Cover: Foto ©Andreas Hilbeck / pixelio.de

More available books at **www.hansebooks.com**

HAMILTON'S

DICTIONARY

OF

3,500

MUSICAL TERMS.

BY

JOHN BISHOP.

130th EDITION.

Price One Shilling.

LONDON:

ROBERT COCKS & CO., 6, NEW BURLNGTON ST.

*Music Publishers to Her Most Gracious Majesty Queen Victoria,
and H.R.H. the Prince of Wales.*

THE TIME TABLE.

A ○ is equal to 2 ♩ or 4 ♪ or 8 ♪ or 16 ♪ or 32 ♪ or 64

♩ == 2 ♪ ... 4 ♪ .. 8 ♪ .. 16 ♪ .. 32

♪ == 2 ♪ ... 4 ♪ .. 8 ♪ .. 16

♪ == 2 ♪ ... 4 ♪ .. 8

♪ == 2 ♪ ... 4

♪ == 2

HAMILTON's
CELEBRATED DICTIONARY.

COMPRISING AN EXPLANATION OF

3,500

ITALIAN, FRENCH, GERMAN, ENGLISH,

AND OTHER

Musical Terms, Phrases and Abbreviations,

ALSO A

COPIOUS LIST OF MUSICAL CHARACTERS,

SUCH AS ARE FOUND IN THE WORKS OF

Adam, Aguado, Albrechtsberger Auber, Bach (J. S.), Baillot, Beethoven, Bellini, Berbiguier, Bertini, Burgmuller, Bishop (John), Bochsa, Brunner, Briccialdi, Campagnoli, Carulli, Chopin, Choron, Chaulieu, Cherubini, Clarke (J.) Clementi, Cramer, Croisez, Czerny, De Beriot, Diabelli, Dœhler, Donizetti, Dotzauer, Dreyschock, Drouet, Dussek. Fétis, Field, Forde, Gabrielsky, Giuliani, Gorla, Haydn, Handel, Herold, Herz, Herzog, Horsley, Hummel, Hunten, Haensel, Henselt, Kalkbrenner, Kuhe, Kuhlau, Kreutzer, Koch, Lanner, Labitzky, Lafont, Lemke, Lemoine, Liszt, Labarre, Marpurg, Mareailhou, Mayseder, Meyerbeer, Mercadante, Mendelssohn, Moscheles. Mozart, Musard, Nicholson, Nixon, Osborne, Onslow, Pacini, Pixis, Plachy. Rameau, Reicha, Rinck, Rosellen, Romberg (A. and B.), Rossini, Rode. Rousseau, Ricci, Reissiger, Schmitt (A.), Schubert (C.), Schulhoff, Sor, Spohr, Strauss, Santos (D. J. Dos), Thalberg, Tulou, Viotti, Wallace (W. V.), Warren, Walckier, Weber, Wesley (S. S.), &c.

WITH

AN APPENDIX,

CONSISTING OF A REPRINT OF

JOHN TINCTOR'S "TERMINORUM MUSICÆ DIFFINITORIUM,"

The First Musical Dictionary known.

EDITED BY

JOHN BISHOP,

OF CHELTENHAM.

LONDON:

ROBERT COCKS & CO. NEW BURLINGTON STREET,

MUSIC PUBLISHERS TO HER MOST GRACIOUS MAJESTY QUEEN VICTORIA, AND HIS IMPERIAL MAJESTY NAPOLEON THE THIRD,

AND MESSRS SIMPKIN, MARSHALL, AND CO.

STATIONERS' HALL COURT

ADVERTISEMENT

TO THE THIRTY-SECOND EDITION.

THE extraordinary sale of this little work being a convincing proof of the high opinion entertained of it by the musical public, has induced the publishers to make such additions to it, from time to time, as to secure for it a still increasing celebrity and place it far beyond the reach of competition.

They have had all the terms contained in the former Appendix inserted in their proper places in the body of the work, and have besides introduced several hundred additional terms, and extended the lists of phrases and abbreviations. They have further introduced a reprint of the first Musical Dictionary known, which they trust will render this truly *unique* book as acceptable to the learned musician as it has already proved itself to have been to the beginner, for whose use it was primarily designed.

New Burlington Street, London, W

NOTICE.

This work may be ordered of any Musicseller or Bookseller; but inasmuch as several spurious imitations have from time to time appeared, it will be necessary (for those who wish to secure the genuine work) to specify in their orders the name of the Author and also of the Publisher. Orders must be given for " Hamilton's Dictionary of 3,500 Musical Terms," published by ROBERT COCKS and Co., New Burlington Street, London. W.

TEACHERS AND AMATEURS OF MUSIC.

LADIES AND GENTLEMEN,

I once more have the honour of appearing before you and in so doing I beg to return my most sincere and respectful thanks for the kind patronage you have been pleased to extend to my Elementary Musical Works published by Messrs. R. Cocks and Co.

Within the last few years thirty-one editions of my Dictionary have been sold. This THIRTY-SECOND, new and much enlarged edition will be found to comprise 3,500 words; and I think I may venture to challenge all Europe to produce any similar work, equally extensive and complete, and at such an incredibly low price.

The utility of a Musical Dictionary to the Professor the Amateur, and particularly the Pupil, is sufficiently obvious in the present highly cultivated state of the science; and I do hope that this work, and my NEW MUSICAL GRAMMAR, will shortly be considered as indispensable to the formation of the Professor and the Amateur of the delightful art, as are Murray's Grammar and Johnson's Dictionary to the Student of English Literature.

As several Teachers have objected to the introduction of German musical terms into this work, the Author begs to say, that since this is merely a work for reference, he imagines that it cannot well be v complete.

The German words inserted are such only as occu. o titles, o in the course of musical works printed in that country, and of which the proper significations are not to be found in the ordinary German and English Dictionaries.

I remain, Ladies and Gentlemen,
Your grateful and obedient Servant,

LONDON, 1849.   J. A. HAMILTON.

"There are many hundreds of words in this Dictionary that I cannot find in others which cost me ten times more money; and, what is more to the purpose, they are words or terms which are daily used in the higher musical circles."— *Vide the Cheltenham Looker-on, No. 11, 3rd Series.*

DICTIONARY

OF

MUSICAL TERMS.

A

A. (*Italian*) By, for, at, &c.; as, *à piacere*, at pleasure.

ABBANDONASI (*Italian.*)
ABBANDONATAMENTE (*Italian*).
ABBANDONO, con (*Italian.*)
ABANDON, *à l'* (*French.*)
} With self-abandonment; despondingly.

ABBASSIMENTO DI MANO (*Italian*). Fall of the hand in beating time.

ABBELLIMENTI (*Italian plural*). Ornaments; embellishments.

ABBREVIATURE (*Italian plural*).
ABKÜRZUNGEN (*German plural*).
} Abbreviations.

A BATTUTA (*Italian*). In strict or measured time.

A BENE PLACITO (*Italian*). At pleasure as to time.

ABSATZ (*German*). A section, or musical sentence.

ABSETZEN (*German*).
ABSTOSSEN (*German*).
} These words imply a style of performance similar to that indicated by the Italian word *Staccato*.

ABWECHSELND (*German*). *Alternating;* as *mit abwechselnden Manualen*, alternately from the great to the choir organ, &c.

ACADEMIE ROYALE DE MUSIQUE (*French*). The name given to the French Opera-house.

A CAPPELLA (*Italian*). In the church style.

A CAPRICCIO (*Italian*). At will, agreeable to our fancy.

ACATHISTUS. A hymn sung in the ancient Greek Church in honour of the Virgin.

ACCADEMIA (*Italian*). A concert.

ACCELERANDO (*Italian*). With gradually increasing velocity of movement.

ACCELERATO (*Italian*). Accelerated, increased in rapidity.

ACCENT. A slight stress placed upon a note to mark its place and relative importance in the bar.

ACCENTUARE (*Italian*). To accentuate; to perform with expressive accentuation.

ACCIACCATURA (*Italian*). A species of arpeggio.

ACCIDENTS. Occasional sharps, flats, and naturals placed before notes in the course of a piece.

ACCOLADE (*French*). The *brace* employed to connect two or more staves in pianoforte or harp music, and in scores,

ACCOMPAGNAMENTO (*Italian*). } An accompaniment.
ACCOMPAGNEMENT (*French*). }

ACCOMPAGNEMENS (*French plural*). Accompaniments.

ACCOMPAGNATORE (*Italian*). } An accompanist.
ACCOMPAGNATEUR (*French*). }

ACCOMPANIMENT. A part added to a principal, by way of enhancing the effect of the composition. Accompaniments are sometimes *ad libitum*, that is, they may be dispensed with in the performance; and sometimes *obbligato*, that is, indispensable to the proper effect of the whole.

ACCORD. (*French*). A chord.

ACCORDARE (*Italian*). To tune.

ACCORDA TO (*Italian*). Tuning.

ACCORDATORE (*Italian*). } A tuner.
ACCORDEUR (*French*). }

ACCORDATURA (*Italian*). The scale of notes, according to which the open strings of any instrument are tuned. Thus, C, G, D, A, form the accordatura of the tenor and of the violoncello; G, D, A, E, that of the violin; E, A, D. G, B, E, that of the guitar, &c.

ACCORDER (*French*). To tune an instrument.

ACCORDO (*Italian*). A chord.

ACCRESCIUTO (*Italian*). Augmented, in speaking of intervals.

ACCRESCIMENTO (*Italian*). An increase, or augmentation.

ACHTELNOTE (*German*, A quaver.

A CHULA. A Portuguese dance resembling the Fandango.

A CINQUE (*Italian*). For five voices or instruments.

ACOUSTICS. The general theory of sound.

ACTE DE CADENCE (*French*). A cadence.

ACUTE. High as to pitch; elevated in the general scale c. sounds.

ADAGIO (*Italian*). A very slow degree of movement, demanding much taste and expression in the performance.

ADAGIO ASSAI or MOLTO (*Italian*). Very slow and expressive.

ADAGIO CANTABILE E SOSTENUTO (*Italian*). Very slow, singing, and sustained.

ADAGIO PATETICO (*Italian*). Slow, with pathetic expression.

ADAGISSIMO (*Italian*). Extremely slow.

ADDITATO (*Italian*). Fingered.

ADDITIONAL KEYS. The keys of a pianoforte or other instrument which extend beyond F in alt.

A DEMI VOIX (*French*). } Synonymous with *mezza voce*.
A DEMI JEU (*French*). } see that term.

A DEUX TEMPS (*French*). Two equal times or measure-notes in a bar.

A DEUX (*French*). For two voices or instruments.

ADJUNCT NOTES. Unaccented auxiliary notes.

AD LIBITUM (*Latin*). *At will, or discretion.* This expression implies that the time of some particular passage is left to the pleasure of the performer; or that he is at liberty to introduce whatever embellishments his fancy may suggest.

ADORNAMENTO (*Italian*). An ornament.

A DUE (*Italian*). For two voices or instruments.

A DUR (*German*). The Key of A major.

ÆQUISONANS } Of the same or like sound; an unison.
ÆQUISONANT }

ÆSTHETICS (*From the Greek*). The doctrine of taste as applied to the fine arts.

A EUSSERSTE STIMMEN (*German plural*). The extreme parts.

AFFANNOSO, con (*Italian*). With mournful expression.

AFFETTUOSO (*Italian*).
AFFETTUOSAMENTE (*Italian*.) } With tenderness and pathos.
AFFETTO, con (*Italian*).

AFFLIZIONE, con (*Italian*). Sorrowfully, with affliction.

AFFRETTANDO (*Italian*). } Accelerating, hurrying the
AFFRETTATE (*Italian*). } time.

A FOFA. A Portuguese dance resembling the Fandango.

AGEVOLE (*Italian*), Without labour, light, easy, agreeably

AGILITA, con (*Italian*). With lightness and agility.

AGITATO (*Italian*).
AGITAZIONE, con (*Italian*). } With agitation, anxiously

AGNUS DEI (*Latin*). One of the principal movements of the mass

A GRAND CHŒUR (*French*). For the full chorus, in opposition to the passages for the soli parts only.

A GRAND ORCHESTRE (*French*). For the full orchestra

AGREMENS (*French plural*). Embellishments.

AIR (*French*). An air, or song; as *Air Ecossois*, a Scotch air.

AIRS TENDRES (*French*). Amatory Airs.

AIS (*German*). A sharp.

A LA MESURE (*French*). In time; synonymous with the Italian words *A tempo*.

ALBERTI BASS. A species of arpeggioed bass, so called from its having been first employed by Domenico Alberti.

A LIVRE OUVERT (*French*). This phrase signifies to perform a piece of music at first sight.

ALLIEVO (*Italian*). A pupil.

AL (*Italian*).
ALLO (*Italian*).
ALL' (*Italian*). } *To the*; sometimes, *in the style of.*
ALLA (*Italian*).

ALLA BREVE (*Italian*). A quick species of common time, formerly used in church music.

ALLA CACCIA. In the hunting style.

———— CAPPELLA. In the church style.

———— MARCIA. In the march style.

———— MODERNA. In the modern style.

———— MILITARE. In the military style.

———— POLACCA. In the style of a Polish dance.

———— RUSSE. In the style of Russian music.

———— SICILIANA. In the style of the Sicilian shepherd' dance.

———— SCOZZESE. In the Scotch style.

———— TEDESCA. In the German style

———— TURCA. In the Turkish style.

ALLA VENEZIANA. In the Venetian style.

——— ZOPPA. In a constrained and limping style

——— STRETTA (*Italian*). Increasing the time; accelerating the degree of movement.

ALL' ANTICA. In the ancient style.

——— ESPAGNUOLA. In the Spanish style.

——— INGLESE. In the English style.

——— ITALIANA. In the Italian style.

ALLEGRAMENTE (*Italian*). With quickness.

ALLEGRETTO (*Italian*). Somewhat cheerful, but not so quick as *Allegro*.

ALLEGRETTO SCHERZANDO (*Italian*). Moderately playful and vivacious.

ALLEGREZZA (*Italian*). *Joy :* as, *con allegrezza*, joyfully, animatedly.

ALLEGRISSIMO (*Italian*). Extremely quick and lively.

ALLEGRO (*Italian*). *Quick, lively.* A term implying a rapid and vivacious movement, but which is frequently modified by the addition of other words: as,

ALLEGRO AGITATO. Quick, with anxiety and agitation

——— ASSAI. Very quick.

——— COMODO. With a convenient degree of quickness.

——— CON BRIO. Quick, with brilliancy.

——— CON FUOCO. Quick, with fire.

——— CON MOTO. Quick, with more than the usual degree of movement.

——— CON SPIRITO. Quick, with spirit

——— DI BRAVURA. Quick, dashing and brilliant

——— FURIOSO. Quick, with fury.

——— MA GRAZIOSO. Quick, but gracefully.

——— MA NON TROPPO. ⎫ Quick, but not to ex
——— MA NON PRESTO. ⎭ cess.

ALLEGRO MOLTO, or DI MOLTO. Very quick

———————— VELOCE. Quick, with rapidity.

———————— VIVACE. With vivacity.

———————— VIVO. Quick, with unusual briskness.

ALLEMANDE (*French*). A dance peculiar to Germany and Switzerland.

ALL' IMPROVVISTA (*Italian*). ⎱ Extemporaneously, with-
ALL' IMPROVVISO (*Italian*). ⎰ out premeditation.

AL LOCO (*Italian*). To some previous place; a term of reference.

ALLONGER (*French*). *To lengthen:* as *allongez l'archet* lengthen the stroke of the bow.

ALL' OTTAVA (*Italian*). *In the octave.* An expression often met with in scores, to signify that one part is to play an octave above or below another.

ALL' UNISONO (*Italian*). In unison, or sometimes, by extension, in octaves.

ALMA REDEMPTORIS (*Latin*). A hymn to the Virgin.

AL RIGORE DI TEMPO (*Italian*). In strict time.

AL ROVESCIO (*Italian*). By reverse or contrary motion.

AL SEGNO,
AL SEG. (*abbrev.*) ⎱ Or the character 𝄋 signifies that the performer must return to a similar character in the course of the movement, and play from that place to the word *fine*, or the mark ⌢ over a double bar.

ALT. (*abbrev*). ⎱ High in the scale of sounds—*Ottava Alta*,
ALTA (*Italian*). ⎰ an octave higher.

ALTERATIO (*Latin*). A term formerly applied to the doubling the value of a note.

ALTERATO (*Italian*). ⎱ Augmented, with respect to in-
ALTERÉ (*French*). ⎰ tervals.

ALTERNATIVO (*Italian*). Alternating; proceeding alternately from one movement to another.

ALTISSIMO (*Italian*). Extremely high as to pitch.

ALTISTA (*Italian*). } One who has an *alto* or *counter-tenor*
ALTISTE (*French*). } voice.

ALT-GEIGE (*German*). } The tenor violin.
ALT-VIOLE (*German*). }

ALTO (*Italian*). In vocal music, indicates the counter-tenor,
or highest male voice. It also indicates the part for the
tenor in instrumental music.

ALTO CLEF. The C clef on the third line of the stave.

ALTRA (*Italian*). } Other.
ALTRO (*Italian*). }

ALTRI (*Italian plur.*). Others.

ALT-SCHLUSSEL (*German*). } The C clef on the third
ALT-ZEICHEN (*German*). } line.

ALZAMENTE DI MANO (*Italian*). The elevation of the
hand in beating time.

AMABILE (*Italian*). } Amiably.
AMABILITA, *con* (*Italian*). }

AMAREZZA, *con* (*Italian*). With bitterness and affliction.

AMATEUR (*French*). A non-professional lover of music.

AMBROSIAN CHANT. The chant introduced by St
Ambrose into the church at Milan, in the fourth century.

AMBUBAJE. This, among the ancient Greeks, was the
name of a society of strolling flute-players.

AME (*French*). The sound-post of a violin, tenor, &c.

A MEZZA VOCE (*Italian*). In a subdued tone.

A MOLL (*German*). The key of A minor.

AMOREVOLMENTE (*Italian*). With extreme affection.

AMOROSAMENTE (*Italian*). In a tender and affectionate
manner.

AMOROSO (*Italian*).
AMOREVOLE (*Italian*). } Affectionately, tenderly.
AMORE, *con* (*Italian*).

AMPHIMACER. A musical foot, composed of one long one short, and one long note.

AMPHIBRACH. A musical foot, comprising one short, one long, and one short note.

ANACREONTIC. In the Bacchanalian style.

ANALYSE (*French*). An analysis.

ANAPEST. A musical foot, containing two short notes and a long one.

ANAPHORA. This term formerly signified the immediate repetition of a passage.

ANCORA (*Italian*). Again, once more.

ANCHE (*French*). The reed or mouth-piece of the oboe, clarionet, &c.

ANCIA (*Italian*). The reed of the oboe, bassoon, &c.

ANDAMENTO (*Italian*). An accessary idea or episode in a fugue.

ANDANTE (*Italian*). Implies a movement somewhat slow and sedate, but in a gentle and soothing style. This term is often modified, both as to time and style, by the addition of other words; as,

ANDANTE AFFETTUOSO. Slow, but pathetically.
———— CANTABILE. Slow, but in a singing style.
———— CON MOTO. Slow, but with emotion.
———— GRAZIOSO. Slow, but gracefully.
———— MAESTOSO. Slow, with majesty.
———— NON TROPPO. Slow, but not too much so.
———— PASTORALE. Slow, and with pastoral simplicity.

ANDANTINO (*Italian*). Somewhat slower than *Andante*

ANFANGSGRÜNDE (*German*) The elements or principles.

ANFANGS RITORNELL (*German*). An introductory symphony to an air, &c.

ANGLAISE (*French*). A tune adapted for a country dance, in the English style.

ANGOSCIAMENTO, *con* (*Italian*). With anxiety, apprehensively.

ANHALTENDE CADENZ (*German*). A pedal note or organ-point.

ANHANG (*German*). An adjunctive member to a musical sentence; a sort of coda.

ANIMA, *con* (*Italian*).
ANIMATO (*Italian*).
ANIMOSO (*Italian*).
} With animation, in a spirited manner.

ANLAGE (*German*). The plan or outline of a composition.

ANLEITUNG (*German*). An introduction; this term often occurs in the titles to German publications.

ANONER (*French.*) To perform in a hesitating manner.

ANSATZ (*German*). The mouth-piece of a wind instrument.

ANSCHLAG (*German*). The percussion of a discord.

ANSPRACHE (*German*). Intonation.

ANTECEDENT. The subject of a fugue, or of a point of imitation.

ANTHEM. A composition in the sacred style, the words of which are generally selected from the Psalms.

ANTIBACCHIUS. A musical foot composed of two long notes and a short one.

ANTICIPATION.
ANTICIPAZIONE (*Italian*).
} A taking of a note or chord previous to its natural and expected place.

ANTICO, *all'* (*Italian*). In the ancient style

ANTIPHONE. Responses made by one part of the choir to another, or by the congregation to the priest, in the Catholic divine service.

APERTO (*Italian*). *Open;* an adjective sometimes used to indicate the employment of the *damper pedal.*

A PIACERE (*Italian*). ⎫ At the pleasure of the per-
A PIACIMENTO (*Italian*). ⎭ former. See *Ad libitum.*

A PLOMB (*French.*) With exactitude as to time.

A POCO A POCO (*Italian*). By degrees; by little and little.

A POCO PIU LENTO (*Italian*). A little slower.

A POCO PIU MOSSO (*Italian*). A little quicker

APPASSIONATO (*Italian*). ⎫
APPASSIONAMENTO (*Italian*). ⎬ With intensity of feeling.
APPASSIONATAMENTE (*Italian*). ⎭

APPLICATUR (*German*). A position or shift on the violin, violoncello, &c.

APPOGGIATURA (*Italian*). A note of embellishment, generally written in a small character.

APPOGGIATO (*Italian*). Dwelt, leaned upon.

A QUATRE MAINS (*French*). ⎫ For four hands A piano-
A QUATRO MANI (*Italian*). ⎭ forte duet.

A QUATTRO (*Italian.*) For four voices or instruments.

ARCATO (*Italian*). Bowed, played with the bow.

ARCHEGGIAMENTO (*Italian*) The management of the bow, in playing the violin, &c.

ARCHET (*French*). The bow.

ARCO, (*Italian*) The bow. In violin, violoncello, and tenor music, *Arco,* or *Coll' Arco,* implies that the notes are again to be played with the bow, instead of *Pizzicato,* that is, twitched by the fingers.

ARCHLUTE. } A stringed instrument resembling
ARCHILUTH (*French*). } the Theorbo, and by some con
ARCILIUTO (*Italian*). } sidered synonymous with it.

ARDITO (*Italian*). Boldly, energetically.

ARETINIAN SYLLABLES. The syllables *ut, re, mi, fa. sol, la,* used by Guido d'Arezzo for his system of hexachords.

ARIA (*Italian*). An air or song. There are several species of airs; as,

ARIA BUFFA. A comic air.

———— D'ABILITA. An air of difficult execution.

———— CONCERTATA. An air with elaborate orchestral accompaniments.

———— DI BRAVURA. An air requiring great volubility of execution.

———— DI CANTABILE. An air in a graceful, singing and flowing style.

———— FUGATA. An air, the accompaniments to which are written in the fugue style.

———— PARLANTE. An air more declamatory than melodious.

———— TEDESCA. An air in the German style.

ARIE AGIUNTE (*Italian plu.*). Airs added to, or introduced in any opera, on subsequent performances.

ARIETTA (*Italian*). } A short air or melody.
ARIETTINA (*Italian*). }

ARIETTA ALLA VENEZIANA (*Italian*). Little airs in the style of the Venetian Barcarolles.

ARIOSO (*Italian*). In the style of an air; vocal, melodious.

ARMER LA CLEF (*French*). This expression relates to the placing of the sharps or flats requisite for the key of the piece immediately after the clef.

ARMONIA (*Italian*). Harmony.

ARMONICA (*Italian*). A musical instrument, generally constructed of glass.

ARMONIOSO (*Italian*). } Harmoniously.
ARMONIOSAMENTE (*Italian*). }

ARMONISTA (*Italian*). One who understands harmony.

ARPA (*Italian*). The harp.

ARPA DOPPIA (*Italian*). The double-action harp.

ARPEGGIANDO (*Italian*). ⎫ Passages formed of the notes
ARPEGGIATO (*Italian*). ⎬ of chords taken in rapid
ARPEGGIO (*Italian*). ⎭ succession, in imitation of
the harp, are said to be in *Arpeggio*. The employment
of either term also signifies that certain chords are to be so
played.

ARSIS and THESIS (*Greek*). The elevation and depression
of the hand in beating time.

ART DE L'ARCHET (*French.*) The art of bowing.

ARTICOLARE (*Italian*). To articulate all the notes distinctly.

ARTICOLATO (*Italian*). Articulated, distinctly enounced.

ARTISTA (*Italian*). ⎫ *An artist.* As a musical term, this is
ARTISTE (*French*). ⎭ usually applied only to first-rate performers or composers.

AS (*German*). A flat: as,

AS DUR. A flat major.

AS MOLL. A flat minor.

ASPERGES ME (*Latin*). The opening of the mass.

ASPREZZA (*Italian*). With dryness, coarsely.

ASSAI (*Italian*). *Very, extremely.* This adverb is always
joined to some other word, of which it extends the signification: as, *Adagio assai,* very slow; *Allegro assai,* very quick.

A SUO ARBITRIO (*Italian*). ⎫ Synonymous terms with *ad*
A SUO COMMODO (*Italian*). ⎭ *libitum;* indicating that
the time, &c. are left to the will of the performer.

A TABLE SEC (*French*). A term relating to the practice
of vocal exercises unaccompanied by an instrument.

A TEMPO (*Italian*). } *In time.* A term used to denote
A TEM. (*abbrev.*) } that, after some short relaxation
in the time, the performer must return to the original
degree of movement.

A TEMPO DI GAVOTTA (*Italian*). In the time of a
gavot; moderately quick.

A TEMPO GIUSTO (*Italian*). In strict and equal time.

A TEMPO ORDINARIO (*Italian*) In an ordinary or
moderate degree of movement.

A TRE, or A 3 (*Italian*). } For three voices or instru
A TROIS (*French*). } ments.

ATTACCA (*Italian*). } Implies that the performer
ATTACCA SUBITO (*Italian*). } must directly commence
the following movement.

ATTACCATO SUBITO (*Italian*). To be commenced immediately.

ATTENDANT KEYS. The relative key; the key of the dominant and its relative, and of the subdominant and its relative

ATTO (*Italian*). Any act of an opera; as *Atto primo, Atto*
secondo—act the first, act the second.

ATTORI (*Italian plur. mas.*). } The principal singers in
ATTRICE (*Italian plur. fem.*). } an opera.

AUBADE (*French*). A morning concert given in the open air.

AUDACE, *con* (*Italian*). With boldness.

AUFHALTUNG (*German*). A suspension.

AUFLOSUNG (*German*). The resolution of a discord.

AUFSCHLAG (*German*). The unaccented part o. a bar.

AUFSTRICH (*German*). An up-bow.

AUFTAKT (*German*). See AUFSCHLAG.

AUGMENTATION. In counterpoint and fugue this term
implies that a subject is imitated in notes of greater length.*

---

* See Cherubini's Course of Counterpoint and Fugue. in 2 vols. 8vo.,
Second Edition, published by Messrs Cocks and Co., price 15s.

AUGMENTED INTERVALS. Those which are a semitone greater than major or perfect intervals.

A UNA CORDA (*Italian*). On one string.

AUS (*German*). *From, out of;* occurs in German titles, &c.

AUSARBEITUNG (*German*). The elaboration or last finish of a musical composition.

AUSDEHNUNG (*German*). Extension, expansion.

AUSDRUCK (*German*). Expression.

AUSFÜHRUNG (*German*). Performance.

AUSHALTUNG (*German*). The sustaining a note.

AUSHALTUNGSZEICHEN (*German*). The character called a *pause.*

AUSWEICHUNG (*German*). Modulation.

AUTENTICO (*Italian*). Authentic.

AUTHENTIC. A name given to those *church modes* whose melody was confined within the limits of the tonic (or final) and its octave.

AUTHENTIC CADENCE. A perfect cadence.

AUXILIARY NOTES. Those standing on the next degree above or below an essential note when they do not proceed from one essential note to another.

AUXILIARY SCALES. The scales of the attendant or relative keys are so called by some authors.

AVE MARIA (*Latin*). A hymn to the Virgin.

A VISTA (*Italian*). At sight, *a prima vista*, at first sight.

AZIONE SACRA (*Italian*). A sacred drama.

B.

BACCHIA. A Kamschatdale dance, in $\frac{2}{4}$ time.

BACCHIUS. A musical foot consisting of one short and two long notes.

BACCIOCOLO (*Italian*). A musical instrument common in some parts of Tuscany.

BACHELOR OF MUSIC. The first musical degree taken at our universities. Abbreviated, *Mus. Bac.*

BADINAGE (*French.*) Playfulness.

BAISSER (*French*). To lower or flatten in pitch.

BALKEN (*German*). The bass-bar of a violin, &c.

BALLAD. A short and familiar song.

BALLATA (*Italian*).
BALLATETTA (*Italian.*) } A ballad.

BALLET (*French*). } A theatrical representation of some
BALLETTO (*Italian*). } story or fable, by means of dance or metrical action, accompanied with music. In England, the second or concluding piece of the evening's entertainment at the Italian Opera House is generally a ballet.

BALLET-MASTER. The artist whose province it is to superintend the rehearsals and performance of the ballet; and who not unfrequently invents the fable and its details himself.

BALLI INGLESI (*Italian plu.*) English country dances.

BALLI DELLA STIRIA (*Italian plu.*). Styrian dances resembling waltzes.

BALLI UNGARESI (*Italian plu.*). Hungarian dances in $\frac{2}{4}$ time, usually accented on the weak part of the bar.

BALLO (*Italian*). A dance, or dance tune.

BANDA (*Italian*). A band.

BANDORE. } An ancient stringed instrument of
BANDORA (*Italian*). } the lute species.

BAR. Lines drawn across the stave to divide the music in small and equal portions of duration; each of these small portions in themselves is also called a *bar*.

BARCAROLLE (*Italian*). Airs sung by the Venetian Gondoliers, or boatmen, while following their avocations. These melodies possess a simple and artless beauty, equally delightful to the unpractised and to the most cultivated ear.

BARD. A poet and musician.

BARITONE CLEF. The F clef placed on the third line.

BARITON (*French*). ⎫ A male voice, intermediate, in re-
BARITONE. ⎬ spect to pitch, between the base
BARITONO (*Italian*). ⎭ and the tenor voices. Ph;llips
and Tamburini are fine examples of this species of voice.

BAROCO (*Italian*). ⎫ Terms applied to music having a
BAROQUE (*French*). ⎭ confused harmony, an unnatura.
melody, and full of modulations and discords.

BARRÉ (*French*). In guitar playing, a temporary nut,
formed by placing the fore-finger of the left hand across the
strings.

BARRE DE MESURE (*French*). A bar-line.

BARRE DE REPETITION (*French*). A dotted double bar.

BAS-DESSUS (*French*). *mezzo-soprano* or second treble
voice.

BASE. The lowest part in a musical composition.

BASSA (*Italian*). Low ; ——— *Ottava bassa* (or *8va bassa*),
an octave lower.

BASS. The lowest part in a musical composition.

BASSE (*French*). The bass part, whether vocal or instrumental

——— CHANTANTE (*French*). The vocal bass.

——— CHIFFREE (*French*). The figured bass.

——– CONTRAINTE (*French*). A ground-bass.

——— FONDAMENTALE (*French*). The fundamenta'
bass.

——— FIGUREE (*French*). The figured bass.

BASSETTO (*Italian*). The little bass.

BASSGEIGE (*German*). The violoncello.

BASSO (*Italian*). The base part, vocal or instrumental.

——— BUFFO (*Italian*). A bass singer in a comic opera

——— CANTANTE (*Italian*). The vocal bass.

——— CONCERTANTE. The principal bass.

——— CONTINUO. The continued bass.

BASSO FIGURATO (*Italian*).   The figured bass.
—— FONDAMENTALE (*Italian*). The fundamental bass
—— NUMERATO (*Italian*).   The figured bass.
—— OSTINATO (*Italian*).   A ground-bass.
—— RIPIENO.   The bass of the full or tutti parts.
BASSON (*French*).   A bassoon.
BASS-SCHLÜSSEL (*German*). ⎫
BASS-ZEICHEN (*German*).   ⎬ The bass clef.
BASTANTE (*Italian*).   Enough ; sufficient.
BATON DE MESURE (*French*).   The roll of paper or
other material with which the conductor of an orchestra
marks the time.
BATTEMENT (*French*).   ⎱ That species of shake called a
BATTIMENTO (*Italian*). ⎰   beat.
BATTRE LA MESURE (*French*).   To mark the time by
beating with the hand or with a stick, &c.   To beat time.
BATTUTA (*Italian*).   Time ; the accented part of the bar.
BAU (*German*).   The *structure*, speaking of musical instru-
ments, &c.*
B CANCELLATUM (*Latin*).   A sharp (♯).
B DUR (*German*).   The key of B flat major.
BEAT.   One of the principal graces in music.
BEATING TIME.   Marking the divisions of the bar by
means of the hand or foot.
BECARRE (*French*).   A natural (♮).
BEC (*French*).) ⎫
BECCO (*Italian*).⎬ The mouth-piece of a clarionet.
BECCO POLACCO (*Italian*).   The name of a large spe-
cies of bagpipe used in some parts of Italy.
BEGEISTERUNG (*German*)   Exaltation, excitement, poet-
ical enthusiasm.

---

* See Otto's Treatise on the Structure and Preservation of the Violin
and all bow instruments. enlarged by J. Bishop, price 3s.

BEGLEITENDÆ STIMMEN (*German plur.*) The accom
panying parts.

BEGLEITER (*German*). An accompanist.

BEGLEITUNG (*German*). An accompaniment.

BELL of a trumpet, horn, &c., is the wide lower opening a'
which the sound is emitted.

BELLEZZA, con (*Italian*). With beauty of expression.

BELLICOSAMENTE (*Italian*). In a martial style.

BELL METRONOME. A metronome with the addition of
a small bell which strikes at the commencement of each
bar.*

BEMOLISER (*French*).   } To flatten notes, either at the
BEMOLIZZARE (*Italian*). }   clef or in the course of a
composition.

BEMOL (*French*).   } A flat, ($\flat$).
BEMOLLE (*Italian*). }

BEN (*Italian*).   } Well: as,
BENE (*Italian*). }

BENEDICTUS (*Latin*). A movement belonging to a mass,
or Catholic morning service.

BENE PLACITO (*Italian.*) At will.

BEN MARCATO (*Italian*). Well marked. This expression indicates that the passage must be executed in a clear,
distinct, and strongly accented manner

BEQUADRO (*Italian*).   } A natural, ($\natural$).
BEQUARRE (*French*). }

BESCHREIBUNG (*German*). A description.

BEYSPEIL (*German*). An example.

BIANCA (*Italian*). A minim.

BICINIUM (*Latin*). A composition in two parts.

---

* These useful instruments are sold for the Proprietor by Messrs.
Cocks and Co., price 42s.; Metronomes without the bell, price 20s.

BINARY MEASURE. Common time.

BINDUNG (*German*). Syncopation.

BINDUNGSZEICHEN (*German*). A tie or bind.

BIRN (*German*). That part of a clarionet and basset-horn into which the mouthpiece is inserted.

BIS (*Latin*). Twice. A term which indicates that a certain passage, distinguished by a curve drawn over or under it, must be performed *twice*; this abbreviation saves writing the passage over again.

BISCHERO (*Italian*). A peg of a violin, violoncello, &c.

BISCROMA (*Italian*).
BISCROME (*French*). } A semiquaver.

BIS DIAPASON. A double octave.

BIS UNCA. The old name for a semiquaver.

BIZZARO (*Italian*). A term which denotes that the movement to which this is prefixed is written in an irregular and fantastic style.

BLANCHE (*French*). A minim.

BLASEBALGE (*German*). The bellows of an organ.

BLASINSTRUMENT (*German*). A wind instrument.

BLASMUSIK (*German*). Music for wind instruments.

B MOLL (*German*) The key of B flat minor.

BOCAL (*French*).
BOCCHINO (*Italian*). } The mouth-piece of a horn, trombone, or serpent.

BODEN (*German*). The back of a violin, tenor, &c.

BOGEN (*German*). The bow.

BOGENFUHRUNG (*German*). The management of the bow.

BOGENINSTRUMENT (*German*). A bow instrument

BOGENSTRICH (*German*). A stroke of the bow.

BOLERO. A Spanish dance with castanets.

BOMBARDE (*French*).
BOMBARDO (*Italian*). } An old wind-instrument of the hautboy species

BORDONE (*Italian.*) ⎱ The double open diapason stop in an
BOURDON (*French*). ⎰ organ.

BOURREE (*French*). A lively dance in common time be·
ginning with an odd crotchet.

B QUADRATUM (*Latin.*) ⎱ A natural (♮).
B QUADRUM (*Latin*). ⎰

BRANLE (*French*). An old dance.

BRATSCHE (*German*). The tenor violin.

BRAVA, (*Italian feminine*). ⎫ Exclamations of approba-
BRAVI, (*Italian plural*). ⎬ tion used at the Italian
BRAVO, (*Italian masculine*). ⎭ theatres.

BRAVURA (*Italian*). A composition requiring great spirit
and volubility of execution.

BREVE. A note twice the length of the semibreve, seldom
used in modern music.

BRILLANTE (*Italian* and *French*). An expression indi·
·ating a shewy and sparkling style of performance.

BRIO (*Italian*).
BRIOSO (*Italian*). ⎬ With brilliancy and spirit.
BRIO, con (*Italian*).

BRISÉ (*French*). Sprinkled, broken into an arpeggio, in
treating of chords.

BRODERIES (*French*). Embellishments.

B ROTUNDUM (*Latin*). A flat (♭).

BRUSCAMENTE (*Italian*). Abruptly, coarsely.

BUFFA (*Italian*). ⎱ Comic. An actor or singer who takes
BUFFO (*Italian*). ⎰ the light and humorous parts in the
Italian comic opera. This epithet is also applied to the
pieces themselves, as *opera buffa*, a comic opera.

BURLANDO (*Italian.*) Playfully, in a jesting manner.

BURLESCO (*Italian*). With comic and even farcical hu-
mour.

BURLETTA (*Italian*), A light species of musical drama, somewhat in the nature of the English farce.

C.

CABALETTA (*Italian*). A simple melody of a pleasing and attractive character.

CACCIA, *alla* (*Italian*). In the hunting style

CACOPHONY. A discordant combination of sounds, forming no regular harmony.

CADENCE (*French*). A shake; also a cadence in harmony, as *cadence parfaite*, a perfect cadence; *cadence rompue*, an interrupted cadence.

CADENCE. A close in melody or harmony. An ornamental and extemporaneous passage introduced at the close of a song or piece of music.

CADENCE INTERROMPUE (*French*). ⎫ An interrupted
——————— ROMPUE (*French*). ⎬ cadence.
——————— IMPARFAITE (*French*). An imperfect cadence.
——————— PARFAITE (*French*). A perfect cadence.

CADENZA (*Italian*). A cadence, or close, at the termination of a song or other movement, introducing some fanciful and extemporaneous embellishment. In modern music the cadenza is generally written in small notes.

CADENZA D'INGANNO (*Italian*). An interrupted cadence.

CÆSURA (*Latin.*) The rhythmic termination of any passage consisting of more than one musical foot. The last accented note of a phrase, section or period.

CALANDO (*Italian*). Gradually diminishing in tone and quickness; becoming softer and slower by degrees.

CALASCIONE (*Italian*). A species of guitar.

CALCANDO (*Italian.*) Pressing upon, hurrying the time

CALMA, *con* (*Italian*). ⎫ With tranquillity and repose.
CALMATO (*Italian*). ⎭

CALORE, con (*Italian*).
CALOROSO (*Italian*). } With much warm h and animation.

CAMBIARE (*Italian*). To change.

CAMERA (*Italian*). The chamber; as, *musica di camera*, chamber-music.

CAMINANDO (*Italian*). Flowing; with gentle and easy progression.

CAMPANELLA (*Italian*).
CAMPANELLO (*Italian*). } A little bell

CAMPANELLINO (*Italian*). A very little bell.

CANARIE (*French*).
CANARIES. } A sort of jig, in $\frac{3}{8}$ or $\frac{6}{8}$ time.

CANCRIZANS. Retrograde movement.

CANON. A species of uninterrupted imitation.

CANONE (*Italian.*). A canon or catch for several voices or instruments.

CANONE AL SOSPIRO (*Italian*). A canon, the parts of which come in at the distance of a crotchet rest from each other.

CANONE APERTO (*Italian*). An open canon.

——— CHIUSO (*Italian*). A close or hidden canon.

CANTABILE (*Italian*). In a graceful and singing style.

CANTANDO (*Italian*). In a singing manner.

CANTANTE (*Italian*). A part to be executed by the voice.

CANTARE (*Italian*). To sing; as,

CANTARE A ARIA (*Italian*). To sing without confining oneself to the music as written.

CANTARE A ORECCHIO (*Italian*). To sing by ear.

CANTARE DI MANIERA (*Italian.*) To sing with grace and expression.

CANTARE MANIERATA (*Italian*). To sing with a profusion of embellishments, without taste or discernment.

CANTATA (*Italian*). A vocal composition, of several movements, comprising airs and recitatives.

CANTATRICE (*Italian*). A female singer

CANTATILLA (*Italian*). } A short cantata.
CANTATINA (*Italian*). }

CANTICA (*Latin*). } Canticles or devotional songs.
CANTICI (*Italian*). }

CANTICLE. A hymn or divine song.

CANTICUM (*Latin*). A canticle or divine song.

CANTILENA (*Italian*). The melody, air, or principal part in any composition; generally the highest vocal part.

CANTO (*Italian*). The highest vocal part in choral music.

CANTO FERMO (*Italian*). A chant or melody; as also any subject consisting of a few long, plain notes, given as a theme for counterpoint.

CANTO FIGURATO (*Italian*). A figured melody.

———— GREGORIANO (*Italian*). The Gregorian chant.

———— LLANO (*Spanish*). } The plain song or chant.
———— PIANO (*Italian*). }

———— PRIMO (*Italian*). The first treble.

———— SECONDO (*Italian*). The second treble.

CANTOR (*Italian*). } A singer.
CANTORE (*Italian*). }

CANTORIS. A term used in cathedral music* to indicate the passages intended to be taken by those singers who are placed on that side of the building where the *Cantor* or *Precentor* sits; *i. e.* on the left-hand side on entering the choir from the nave.

CANTUS (*Latin*). A song, chant, or melody, as:

CANTUS AMBROSIANUS. The melodies or chants introduced into the church by St. Ambrose.

———— FIRMUS (*Latin*). The plain song, or chant.

———— GREGORIANUS. The chants collected by St. Gregory.

---

* See Warren's splendid edition of Dr. Boyce's Collection of Cathedral Music, 3 vols., folio, price 6 guineas

CANTUS FIGURATUS (*Latin*). Embellis melodies or chants.

CANZONE (*Italian*). An air in two or three parts.

CANZONET (*Italian*)
CANZONETTA (*Italian*). } A short canzone, or song

CAPO (*Italian*). The head or beginning.

CAPOTASTO (*Italian*). The nut of the finger-board of a violin, violoncello, &c.

CAPPELLA, *alla* (*Italian*). In the church sty e.

CAPRICCIETTO (*Italian*). A short capriccio.

CAPRICCIO (*Italian*). A fanciful and irregular species of composition,

CAPRICCIOSO (*Italian*).
CAPRICCIO, *a* (*Italian*). } In a fanciful, capricious styl.

CAPRICE (*French*). A capriccio.

CARATTERE (*Italian*). Character; as, *con molto caratters*, with much character and emphasis.

CAREZZANDO (*Italian*). In a caressing style.

CARICATO (*Italian*). With exaggerated expression.

CARILLONNEUR (*French*). A performer on the carillons.

CARILLONS (*French*). A set of musical bells, or chimes; as also short simple airs adapted for such bells.

CARITÀ, *con* (*Italian*). With tenderness and feeling.

CAROL. The name given to the old ditties sung at Christmas tide.

CASSA GRANDE (*Italian*). The great drum.

CASTANETS.) Pieces of hard wood of a peculiar shape
CASTAGNETS.) which are struck together and used to accompany dance-tunes in Spain and other southern countries.

CASTANETAS, (*Spanish*).
CASTANUELAS (*Spanish*). } The castagnets.

CATCH. A vocal piece in several parts, of a humorous character.

CATENA DI TRILLI (*Italian*). A chain or succession of shakes.

CAVATINA (*Italian*). An air of one movement or part only, occasionally preceded by a recitative.

C BARRÉ (*French*). The character ¢ indicating *alla breve* time.

C DUR (*German*). The key of C major.

CEBELL. The name of an old air written in common time.

CELERE (*Italian*). Quick, rapid.

CELERITÀ, con (*Italian*). With celerity; quick.

CELESTE (*French*). Indicates the employment of the pedal, in some pianofortes, which acts on the celestina stop.

CEMBALO (*Italian*). The harpsichord.

CES (*German*) C flat.

CHACONNE (*French*). An air constructed on a ground bass: a Spanish dance.

CHALUMEAU (*French*). An ancient rustic flute. When this word occurs in music written for the clarionet, it signifies that the passage to which it refers must be played an octave lower.

CHANGEABLE. Said of those chants which may be performed either in the major or minor key of the tonic in which they are written.

CHANGING NOTES. Passing notes on the accented parts of a bar.

CHANSON (*French*). A song.

CHANSONNETTE (*French*). A short or little song.

CHANT. A simple melody, generally harmonised in four parts, to which the daily psalms are sung in cathedrals, &c. See SINGLE CHANT and DOUBLE CHANT.

CHANT (*French*). A song or melody; the vocal part.

CHANT GREGORIEN (*French*). The Gregorian Chant

CHANT SUR LE LIVRE (*French*). A barbarous kind of counterpoint on the plain chant, performed by several voices, each singing extempore.

CHANTANT (*French*). In a singing and melodious style.

CHANTERELLE (*French*). The highest or most acute string of the violin.

CHANTEUR (*French*). A male singer.

CHANTEUSE (*French*). A female singer.

CHASSE (*French*). In the hunting style.

CHE (*Italian*). Than: as, *poco più lento che andante*, rather slower than *andante*.

CHELYS (*Greek*). The lute.

CHEVALET (*French*). The bridge of a violin, tenor, or violoncello.

CHEVILLE (*French*). The peg of a violin, tenor, &c.

CHIAREZZA, con (*Italian*). With clearness and neatness.

CHIARO *Italian*). Clear, as regards sound or tone.

CHIAROSCURO (*Italian*). Light and shade, in modifica tions of *forte* and *piano*.

CHIAVE (*Italian*). A clef.

CHIESA (*Italian*). The church.

CHIFFRES (*French*). Figures, in speaking of thorough-bass.

CHIROGYMNASTE. A square board on which are placed various mechanical contrivances for exercising the fingers of the pianist.

CHIROPLAST. A guide for the hand in pianoforte playing.

CHITARRA (*Italian*). A guitar.

CHIUDENDO (*Italian*). Closing; ending with.

CHŒUR (*French*). The choir, or chorus.

CHORSÄNGER (*German*). A chorus singer.

CHOIR. That portion of a chapel or cathedral set apart for the singers in divine worship; as also the singers themselves taken collectively.

CHOIR-ORGAN.   The smaller or softer toned organ, used to accompany the principal singers in solos, duets, &c.

CHOR (*German*).   Choir, chorus; as, *Arie und Chor*, air and chorus.

CHORAL.   Belonging to the choir; full, or for many voices

CHORAL.   (*German*).   A psalm-tune.

CHORALMÄSSIG (*German.*)   In the style of a psalm-tune.

CHORD.   A combination of several sounds forming harmony

CHORIAMBUS.   A musical foot, accented thus— ⏑⏑ —,

CHORISTER.   A member of the choir.

CHORUS.   A band or company of singers.

CHROMATIC.   Proceeding by semitones, or formed by means of semitones,

CHROMATIQUE (*French*).   Chromatic, proceeding by semitones.

CHURCH MODES.   The ancient modes called by the following names: Dorian, Phrygian, Lydian, Mixolydian, Eolian, Ionian or Iastian.

CIACONNE (*Italian*).   A chaconne; a Spanish dance.

CIMBALLES (*French plu.*).   Cymbals, a military instrument

CIS (*German*).   C sharp; as

—— DUR.   C sharp major.

—— MOLL.   C sharp minor.

CISCIS (*German*).   C double sharp.

CITHARA.   An ancient instrument of the harp kind.

CITOLE.   An instrument of the dulcimer species, and p bably synonymous with it.

CITTERN.   An old instrument resembling the lute.

CIVETTERIA ((*Italian*).   Coquettishly.

CLARIBELLA.   The name of an organ-stop tuned in unison with the Diapasons.

CLARICHORD. | A small keyed instrument of the spinet
CLAVICHORD | kind.

CLARINETTISTA (*Italian*). } A performer on the
CLARINETTISTE (*French*). } rionet.

CLARINETTO (*Italian*). A clarionet.

CLARINO (*Italian*). An octave or small trumpet.

CLARION (*French*). An octave trumpet. Also an organ
stop an octave higher than the trumpet stop.

CLAVECIN (*French.*) }
CLAVICEMBALUM (*Latin*). } The harpsichord.
CLAVICEMBALO (*Italian*). }

CLAVIER (*French, German*). The key-board of a piano or
organ.

CLEF (*French*). A clef.

CLEF DE FA (*French*). The F clef

CLEF DE SOL (*French*). The G clef

CLEF D'UT (*French*). The C clef

CLEFS. Characters used to determine the name and pitch of
the notes; they are of three kinds: treble, tenor, and bass.

CLOCHETTE (*French*). A little bell.

C MOLL (*German*). C minor.

CODA (*Italian*). A few bars added at the close of a composition beyond its natural termination.

CODETTA (*Italian*). A short passage serving to connect
one period or movement with another.

COI (*Italian plur.*). }
COL (*Italian*). }
COLL' (*Italian*). } With the; as col arco, with the bow.
COLLA (*Italian*). }
COLLO, (*Italian*). }

COI VIOLINI (*Italian*). With the violins.

COL BASSO (*Italian*). With the bass.

COL CANTO (*Italian*). } With the melody or voice. These
COLLA VOCE (*Italian*). }   expressions imply that the accompanist must follow the singer in regard to time.

COLLA PARTE (*Italian*). Implies that the accompanist must follow the principal part in regard to time.

COLL' ARCO (*Italian*). With the bow.

COL LEGNO DELL' ARCO (*Italian*). With the bow-stick.

COLOFONIA (*Italian*). }
COLOPHON (*French*). } Resin.

COME (*Italian*). As.

COME PRIMA (*Italian*). As before.

COMES (*Latin*). The answer of a fugue.

COME SOPRA (*Italian*). As above or before.

COME STA (*Italian*). As it stands.

COMMA (*Italian*). A small interval, treated of in the doctrine of musical ratios.

COMMENÇANT (*French*). A beginner in music, &c.

COMMODO, con (*Italian*). }
COMMODAMENTE (*Italian*.) } Quietly, with composure.

COMMON CHORD. A chord consisting of a bass note together with its third and fifth, to which the octave is often added.

COMMON TIMES. Those which have an *even* number of parts in a bar.

COMPIACEVOLE (*Italian*). Pleasing; attractive.

COMPLIN (*Latin*). Evening service, during Lent, in the Catholic Church.

COMPOSITEUR (*French*). }
COMPOSITORE (*Italian*). } A composer.

COMPOSITION. Any musical production is so called. The art of inventing music.

COMPOSIZIONE (*Italian*). A musical composition.

COMPOSIZIONE DI TAVOLINO (*Italian*). Table music, as glees, catches, &c.

COMPOSTO (*Italian*). Composed.

COMPOUND INTERVALS. Such as exceed the extent of an octave.

COMPOUND TIMES. Those measures which contain two or three principal accents; as $\frac{6}{8}$, $\frac{12}{8}$, $\frac{9}{8}$, &c.

CON (*Italian*). With; as,

—— AFFETTO (*Italian*). In an affecting manner.

—— AFFLIZIONE (*Italian*). }
—— AMAREZZA (*Italian*). } With affliction, distress.

—— ANIMA (*Italian*). With animation and feeling.

—— AUDACE (*Italian*). With boldness.

—— BRIO (*Italian*). With brilliancy and spirit.

—— CELERITÀ (*Italian*). With celerity.

CONCENTO (*Italian*). *Concord; agreement.* A selection of pieces is sometimes so called.

CONCENTRARE (*Italian*). To concentrate; to veil the sounds with mystery.

CONCERTANTE (*Italian*). A piece of music for an orchestra, in which several of the instruments have occasional solos. It is also used adjectively, as, *duo concertante*, a duet which each part is alternately principal and subordinate.

CONCERTINA (*Italian*). A small sexangular musical instrument held in the hands. The sounds are produced from metal tongues by pressing the fingers upon the keys which are situated on both sides of the instrument, and at the same time moving the bellows to obtain the necessary supply of wind.

CONCERTINO (*Italian*). This term always denotes a principal part in a concerto, or other full piece; as, *violino primo concertino*, first principal violin: *violino secondo concertino*, second principal violin.

CONCERTO (*Italian*). A composition intended to display the powers of some particular instrument, with orchestral accompaniments.

CONCERTO GROSSO (*Italian*). A composition for many instruments, some principal, some auxiliary.

CONCERTO SPIRITUALE (*Italian*). A miscellaneous concert, chiefly of sacred music.

CONCERT-SPIELER (*German*). A solo-player.

CONCERT-STÜCK (*German*). A concerted piece, a concerto.

CONCINNOUS. Harmonizing; coinciding in effect.

CONCITATO (*Italian*). Perturbed, agitated.

CON COMMODO (*Italian*). In a convenient degree of movement.

CONCORD. An agreeable combination of sounds.

CON DILIGENZA (*Italian*). Diligently, in a studied manner.

—— **DISCREZIONE** (*Italian*). With discretion.

—— **DISPERAZIONE** (*Italian*). With despair.

—— **DOLCEZZA** (*Italian*). With sweetness.

—— **DOLORE** (*Italian*) ⎱ Mournfully, with grief and
—— **DUOLO** (*Italian*). ⎰   pathos.

—— **ELEGANZA** (*Italian*). With elegance.

—— **ENERGIA** (*Italian*). With energy.

—— **ENTUSIASMO** (*Italian*). With enthusiasm

—— **ESPRESSIONE** (*Italian*). With expression.

—— **FACILITÀ** (*Italian*). With facility.

—— **FORZA** (*Italian*). With force; vehemently.

—— **FUOCO** (*Italian*). With fire and animation

CON FURIA (*Italian*). Furiously, with vehemence.

—— FURORE (*Italian*). With agitation and fury.

—— GENTILEZZA (*Italian*). With grace and elegance.

—— GIUSTEZZA (*Italian*). With precision.

—— GRAVITÀ (*Italian*). With gravity.

—— GRAZIA (*Italian*). With grace.

—— GUSTO (*Italian*). With taste.

—— IMPETO (*Italian*). With impetuosity.

—— IMPETO DOLOROSO (*Italian*). With pathetic force and energy.

—— INNOCENZA (*Italian*). In an artless and innocent style.

—— LEGGIEREZZA (*Italian*). With lightness and delicacy.

—— LENTEZZA (*Italian*). With slowness.

—— MODERAZIONE (*Italian*). With a moderate degree of uickness.

—— MOLTO PASSIONE (*Italian*). With great passion and feeling.

—— MOLTO SENTIMENTO (*Italian*). With a high degree of feeling.

—— MORBIDEZZA (*Italian*). With excess of delicacy.

—— MOTO (*Italian*). In an agitated style; with spirit.

—— NEGLIGENZA (*Italian*). Negligently; without restraint.

CONNOISSEUR (*French*). One who possesses a knowledge of, and is a judge of, music.

CON OSSERVANZA (*Italian*). With scrupulous exactness in regard to time.

—— PIACEVOLEZZA (*Italian*). In a pleasing and graceful style.

—— PRECIPITAZIONE (*Italian*). In a hurried manner.

—— PRECISIONE (*Italian*) With distinctness and precision.

CON RESTEZZA (*Italian*). With rapidity.
—— RABBIA (*Italian*). With rage, furiously.
—— RAPIDITÀ (*Italian*). With rapidity
—— RISOLUZIONE (*Italian*). With boldness and reso lution.
—— SDEGNO (*Italian*). In a fiery and indignant style.
CONSECUTIVE. A term applied to a series of similar intervals or chords.
CON SEMPLICITÀ (*Italian*). With simplicity.
—— SENSIBILITÀ (*Italian*). With sensibility and feeling.
—— SENTIMENTO (*Italian*). With feeling and sentiment.
CONSEQUENT. The answer of a fugue or of a point of imitation.
CONSERVATOIRE (*French*). } A public school of music.
CONSERVATORIO (*Italian*). }
CONSOLANTE (*Italian*). In a cheering and encouraging manner.
CON SOLENNITÀ (*Italian*). With solemnity.
CONSONANCE. An interval agreeable to the ear.
CON SONORITÀ (*Italian*). With a full, vibrating kind of tone.
CON SORDINI (*Italian*). With mutes.
—— SPIRITO (*Italian*). With quickness and spirit.
—— SUAVITÀ (*Italian*). With sweetness and delicacy.
—— TENEREZZA (*Italian*). With tenderness.
—— TEPIDITÀ (*Italian*). With coldness and indifference.
—— TIMIDEZZA (*Italian*). With timidity.
CONTINUATO (*Italian*). Continued or held down or on, speaking of notes.
CONTRA-BASSO (*Italian*). The double bass

CONTRA-FAGOTTO (*Italian*). A double bassoon.

CONTRALTO (*Italian*). A counter-tenor voice. The highest species of male voice, and the lowest of female voices.

CONTRAPPUNTISTA (*Italian*). One skilled in counterpoint.

CONTRAPPUNTO (*Italian*). Counterpoint, the first and most necessary step towards a knowledge of musical composition.

———————————— *Sopra il soggetto*, counterpoint above the subject

———————————— *Sotto il soggetto*, counterpoint below the subject.

CONTRAPPUNTO ALLA MENTE (*Italian*). See CHANT SUR LE LIVRE.

———————————— DOPPIO (*Italian*). Double counterpoint.

CONTRAPUNCKT (*German*). Counterpoint.

CONTRAPUNTIST. One who understands counterpoint.

CONTRARY MOTION. Motion in an opposite direction to some other part.

CONTRASSOGGETTO (*Italian*). The counter-subject of a fugue.

CON TRASPORTO (*Italian*, In an angry and passionate manner.

CONTRA VIOLONE (*Italian*). } A double bass.
CONTRE-BASSE (*French*)

CONTRE DANSE (*French*, A quadrille or country dance.

CONTREPOINT (*French*) Counterpoint.

CONTREPOINTISTE (*French*). A contrapuntist.

CONTRESUJET (*French*) The counter-subject of a fugue.

CONTRETEMPS (*French*) Syncopation.

CON VARIAZIONE (*Italian*). With Variations.

CON VEEMENZA (*Italian*). Forcibly, vehemently.

—— VIOLENZA (*Italian*) With violence

—— VIVEZZA (*Italian*). With animation, vivaciously

—— ZELO (*Italian*). With zeal.

COPULA (*Latin*) That movement in an organ by which two rows of keys can be connected together, or the pedals with the keys.

COR (*French*). A horn.

CORALE (*Italian*). The plain chant

CORANTE (*Italian*). A slow dance in $\frac{3}{2}$ or $\frac{3}{4}$ time.

CORDA (*Italian*). ⎫ A string: as, *sopra una corda*, or *sur*
CORDE (*French*). ⎬ *une corde*, on one string

COR DE CHASSE (*French*). A French horn.

COR DE SIGNAL (*French*). A bugle.

CORDIERA (*Italian*). The tail-piece of a violin, tenor, &c

CORIPHŒUS (*Lati*ᵗ The leader of the dances.

CORNAMUSA (*Italian*). The bagpipe.

CORNET. The name of an organ stop consisting of several ranks of pipes.

CORNET (*Italian*) ⎫ A pipe or English flute.
CORNETTO (*Italian*). ⎬

CORNET A PISTONS (*French*). A species of trumpet with valves.

CORNI (*Italian*). The horns.

CORNO (*Italian*). A horn.

CORNO DI BASSETTO (*Italian*) A basset-horn.

———— DI CACCIA (*Italian*). A French horn.

———— INGLESE (*Italian*). An English horn.

CORO (*Italian*). A chorus, or piece for many vo.ces

CORONA (*Italian*) A pause, marked ⌒

CORRENTE (*Italian*). An old dance tune in triple time.

CORYPHÉE (*French*). The leader of the groups of dancers.

COTILLON (*French*). A lively and animated dance in $\frac{6}{8}$ time

COULE (*French*). A group of two notes connected by a slur.

COUNTERPOINT. The art of composition.

COUNTER-TENOR. The highest adult male voice, and the lowest female voice.

———————————— CLEF. The C clef on the third line of the stave.

COUPS D'ARCHET (*French*). Strokes of the bow; ways of bowing.

COURANTE (*French*). An old dance tune in triple time.

COVERED CONSECUTIVES. See HIDDEN CONSECUTIVES.

CREDO (*Latin*). *I believe.* One of the principal movements of the mass.

CREMONA (*Italian*). A small town in Italy, celebrated as having been the residence of the great violin makers, AMATI, STRADUARIUS, GUARNERIUS, &c.

CREMONA. } An organ reed-stop tuned in unison with the
CREMORNE. } diapasons.

CRESCENDO, or CRES. (*Italian*). With a gradually increasing power of tone.

CROCHE (*French*). A quaver.

CROCHET (*French.*) The *hook* of a quaver or other shorter note.

CROOKS. Small curved tubes applied to horns, trumpets &c. to change their pitch.

CROMA (*Italian*). A quaver.

CROMATICA (*Italian*). Chromatic.

CROTCHET. A note equal in duration to one half of minim.

CROWLE. An old English wind instrument

CRUCIFIXUS (*Latin*). Part of the Credo.

CRWTH. A singular Welsh instrument with six strings, and played upon with a bow.

C SCHLÜSSEL (*German*). The C clef.

CUM SANCTO SPIRITU (*Latin*). Part of the Gloria.

CUSTOS (*Latin*). A direct.

CYMEALS. Those metal plates used in military bands, and which on being struck together produce a clashing sound.

D.

DA (*Italian*). By, for, from, &c.

DA CAMERA (*Italian*). In the style of chamber music.

DA CAPELLA (*Italian*). In the church style.

DA CAPO or D. C. (*Italian*). From the beginning. An expression which is often written at the end of a movement, to indicate that the performer must return to and finish with the first strain.

DA CAPO AL FINE (*Italian*). An expression placed at the end of a movement, signifying that the performer must return to the first part, and conclude where the word *Fine* is placed.

DACTYL. A musical foot composed of one long and two short notes.

DACTYLION. A machine invented by H. Herz for strengthening the fingers, and rendering them independent in pianoforte playing.

DAL (*Italian*). By: as *Dal Segno*, from the sign; a mark of repetition.

DAMPER PEDAL That pedal in a pianoforte which raises the dampers from the strings.

DANSE (*French.*) A dance.

DA TEATRO (*Italian*). For the theatre.

DAUER (*German*). The duration or length of notes

D DUR (*German*). D major

DEBILE (*Italian*). } Weakly, feebly.
DEBOLE (*Italian*). }

DECANI. A term employed in cathedral music, implying the passages to which it is affixed must be taken by those singers who are placed on that side of the building where the *Dean* sits: *i. e.* on the right-hand side on entering the choir from the nave.

DECISSIMO (*Italian*). With extreme decision.

DECISO (*Italian*). With decision, boldly.

DECKE (*German*). The belly of a violin, violoncello, &c.

DECORATION (*French*). This occurs in the sense of *signature* in some French works on music.

DECRESCENDO (*Italian*). Gradually decreasing in power of tone.

DEGRE (*French*). A degree of the staff.

DELIBERATAMENTE (*Italian*). } Deliberately.
DELIBERATO (*Italian*). }

DELICATEZZA, *con* (*Italian*). With delicacy of expression.

DELL' (*Italian*). }
DELLA (*Italian*). } Of the.
DELLO (*Italian*). }

DELICATO (*Italian*). }
DELICATEMENTE (*Italian*)· } Delicately.

DELICATISSIMO (*Italian*). With extreme delicacy.

DELYN. The name by which the Welsh call their harp.

DEMANCHER (*French*). To change the position of the hand; to shift on the violin and similar instruments.

DEMI (*French*). A half.

DEMI-CADENCE (*French*) In harmony, a half-cadence, or cadence on the dominant of the key.

DEMI-PAUSE (*French*). A minim rest.

DEMIQUART DE SOUPIR. (*French*). A demisemiquaver rest.

DEMISEMIQUAVER. A short note, equal in duration to one-half the quaver.

DEMI-SOUPIR (*French*). A quaver rest.

DEMI-TON (*French*). A semitone.

DE PROFUNDIS (*Latin*). One of the seven penitential psalms.

DERIVATIVES. Chords derived from others by inversion.

DES (*German*). D flat.

DESCANT. An extemporaneous or other counterpoint on a given subject.

DESCENDANT (*French*). In descending.

DES DUR (*German*). D flat major.

DES MOLL. D flat minor.

DESSUS (*French.*) The treble or upper vocal part.

DESTRA (*Italian*). ⎫ The right hand.
DEXTRA (*Latin*). ⎭

DEUTSCHE FLÖTE (*German*). A German flute.

DEVOZIONE (*Italian*). Devotion; as, *con devozione*, devoutly; with religious feeling.

DI (*Italian*). Of.

DIALOGO (*Italian*). A dialogue. A piece or passage in which two or more parts are so constructed as to respond to one another.

DIAPASON. An octave. A term applied to certain essential stops in an organ, which extend throughout the whole scale of the instrument. Of these there are several sorts: as, *open diapason, stopt diapason, double diapason, &c.*•

DIAPENTE (*Greek*). A perfect fifth.

DIATESSERON (*Greek*). A perfect fourth.

DIATONIC (*Greek*). *Naturally;* that is, according to the degrees of the major or minor scale, or by tones and semitones only.

---

* See Hamilton's Catechism on the Organ, price 1s. also, Hopkins and Rimbault on the Organ, 31s. 6d.

DIESARE (*Italian*). } To sharpen notes, either at the clef
DIÉSER (*French*). } or in the course of a composition.

DIES IRÆ (*Latin*). A principal movement in a requiem.

DIESIS (*Greek*). A small interval used in the mathematical computation of intervals.

DIEZE (*French.*) A sharp ($\sharp$).

DI GRADO (*Italian*). By degrees, in opposition to moving by skips.

DILETTANTE (*French*). A lover of music.

DILUENDO (*Italian*). A gradual dying away of the tone till it arrives at extinction.

DIMINISHED. Somewhat less than perfect, as applied to intervals, chords, &c.

DIMINISHED INTERVALS. Those which are a semitone less than minor or perfect intervals:

DIMINUÉ (*French*). } Diminished, in speaking of inter-
DIMINUITO (*Italian*). } vals.

DIMINUENDO (*Italian*). } This term implies that the
DIM. (*abbrev.*) } quantity or intensity of tone must be gradually diminished.

DIMINUTION. Imitation of a given subject by means of notes of shorter duration.

DI MOLTO (*Italian*). An expression which serves to augment the signification of the word to which it is added; as *allegro di molto*, very quick.

DIRECTEUR (*French*). The director or conductor of a musical performance.

DIRECT MOTION. Similar motion.

DIRGE. A funeral song.

DIS (*German*). D sharp.

DI SALTO (*Italian*). By skips; in opposition to *di grado* which signifies to move by degrees.

DISCANT. See DESCANT. It also implies the upper part.

DISCORD. A dissonant combination of sounds.

DIS-DIAPASON. A double octave.

DIS-MOLL (*German*). D sharp minor.

DISPERATO (*Italian*). } Despairingly; with ex-
DISPERAZIONE, con (*Italian*). } treme emotion.

DISPERSED HARMONY. Harmony in which the notes forming the different chords are separated from each other by wide intervals.

DISSONANCE. An interval or chord displeasing to the ear.

DISSONANT. An inharmonious combination of sounds.

DITO (*Italian*). The finger.

DITONE (*Italian*). } The major third or interval of two
DITONUS (*Latin*). } whole tones.

DIVERTIMENTO (*Italian*). A short, light composition, written in a familiar and pleasing style.

DIVERTISSEMENT (*French*). Certain airs and dances resembling a short ballet, introduced between the acts of the French or Italian opera. Also a composition in a light and pleasing style.

DIVISI (*Italian plu.*) This word is occasionally met with in orchestral parts when a passage is written in octaves or other intervals. It implies that one-half of the performers must play the upper notes, and the others the lower ones.

DIVISION. A series of notes sung to one syllable. Formerly, this term implied a kind of variation upon a given subject.

DIVOTO (*Italian*). Devoutly; in a solemn style.

DIVOZIONE, con (*Italian*). With religious feeling.

D MOLL (*German*). D minor.

DO (*Italian*). A syllable applied in solfaing to the note C

DOCTOR OF MUSIC A degree conferred by one of the Universities. Abbreviated *Mus. Doc.*

DOIGTÉ (*Fronch*). Fingered.

DOIGTER (*French*). The fingering.

DOL. (*abbrev.*) } Implies a soft and sweet style of per-
DOLCE (*Italian*). } formance.

DOLCE MANIERA (*Italian*). A delicate and beautiful style of delivery.

DOLCEMENTE (*Italian*). In a sweet and graceful style.

DOLCEZZA, *con* (*Italian*). With sweetness and softness.

DOLCIANO (*Italian*). }
DOLCINO (*Italian*). } A small bassoon formerly much in
DULCIAN (*French*). } use.
DULCINO (*Italian*). }

DOLCISSIMO (*Italian*). With extreme sweetness.

DOLENTE (*Italian*). }
DOLORE, *con* (*Italian*). } Sorrowfully, pathetically.
DUOLO, *con* (*Italian*). }

DOLENTEMENTE (*Italian*). Dolefully; plaintively.

DOLENTISSIMO (*Italian*). With excess of grief.

DOLOROSAMENTE (*Italian*). } Indicate a soft and pathe-
DOLOROSO (*Italian*). } tic style.

DOMINANT. A name given by theorists to the fifth note of the scale.

DOMINANTE (*French*). The dominant or fifth note of the scale, so called from its governing the key-note in harmony.

DOMINE SALVUM FAC (*Latin*). A prayer for the reigning Sovereign, sung after the mass.

DONA NOBIS PACEM (*Latin*). The concluding movement of the mass or Catholic morning service.

DOPO (*Italian*). After

DOPPEL (*German*). Double; as,

DOPPELGRIFFE (*German.*) Double stop on the violin, &c.

DOPPELSCHLAG (*German*). A turn.

DOPPIO (*Italian*). Double: as,

DOPPIO MOVIMENTO (*Italian*). Double time; that is, as fast again.

DOPPIO TEMPO (*Italian*). Double time.

DORIAN. The name of one of the ancient modes.

DOT. A character which, when placed after a note or rest, increases its duration by the half of its original value.

DOUBLE. An old term for a variation used by Scarlatti and others.

DOUBLE BEMOL (*French*). Double flat.

DOUBLE BAR. Two thick strokes drawn through the staff.

DOUBLE CHANT. A simple harmonized melody extending to *two* verses of a psalm as sung in cathedrals, &c.

DOUBLE COUNTERPOINT. A counterpoint which admits of the parts being inverted.*

DOUBLE CROCHE (*French*). A semiquaver.

DOUBLE DIEZE (*French*). Double sharp.

DOUBLE DRUM. A large drum used in military bands and beaten at both ends.

DOUBLE FUGUE. A fugue on two subjects.

DOUBLE TONGUEING. A mode of articulating quick notes, used by flutists.

DOUBLETTE (*French*). An organ stop, called by us the fifteenth.

DOUX. (*French*). Softly, sweetly.

---

* See Hamilton's Catechism on Double Counterpoint and Fugue.

DRAMA
DRAME (*French*).
DRAMMA (*Italian.*) } A poem accommodated to action. A play, a comedy, a tragedy.

DRAMATIQUE (*French*).
DRAMMATICO (*Italian*). } Dramatic.

DRAMMA BURLESCA (*Italian*). A comic or humorous drama.

DREYKLANG (*German*). A chord of three sounds, a triad

DREYSTIMMIG (*German*). In three parts.

DRITTA (*Italian*). The right hand.

DRIVING NOTES. Long notes placed between shorter ones in the same bar, and accented contrary to the usual rhythmic flow.

DROITE (*French*). Right; as, *maine droite,* right hand.

DRONE. The largest of the three tubes of the bag-pipe. It sounds only one deep note, which serves as a perpetual bass to any tune.

DRUM. A well-known instrument of percussion. Also the tympanum of the ear by which sound is communicated to the auditory nerves.

DRUM-MAJOR. The chief drummer in a regiment.

DUE (*Italian*). In two parts; generally preceded by *a;* as, *a due,* for two.

DUE CORDE (*Italian*). On two strings.

DUE CORI, *à* (*Italian*). For two choirs.

DUETTINO (*Italian*). A short duet.

DUETTO (*Italian*). A duet.

DUE VOLTE (*Italian*). Twice.

DULCIANA. An organ stop, of a soft and sweet quality of tone.

DULCIMER. A triangular chest strung with wires which are struck with a little rod held in each hand.

DUO (*Italian*). A composition for two voices or instruments.

DUOLO, con (*Italian*). With pathos.

DUR (*German*). Major, in relation to keys and modes; as C dur, C major.

DURATE (*Italian*).
DURAMENTE (*Italian*). } Harshly, coarsely
DURO (*Italian*).

DURCHFÜHRUNG (*German*). Development.

DURCHGEHEND (*German*). Transient, passing.

DURÉE (*French*). Length or duration of notes.

DUREZZA (*Italian*). Harshness.

DUTCH CONCERT. A term of ridicule, and applied to cases where each musician plays his own tune, or in his own time.

DUX (*Latin*). The subject of a fugue.

E.

E. } The Italian conjunction *and:* as, *flauto e violino,*
ED. } flute and violin ; *nobilmente ed animato,* with grandeur and spirit.

ECCEDENTE (*Italian*). Augmented, with regard to intervals.

ECCLESIASTICAL MODES. See CHURCH MODES.

ECCO (*Italian*). ⌉ A repetition or imitation of a previous
ECHO (*French*). } passage, with some remarkable modifi-
ECO (*Italian.*) ⌋ cation in regard to tone: this term is often found in organ music.

ECHELLE (*French*). The scale or gamut.

ECLISSES (*French plural*). The sides or hoops of a violin, &c.

ECOLE (*French*). A school or course of instruction.

ECOSSAIS (*French*). ⌉ A dance, tune, or air, in the Scotch
ECOSSAISE (*French.*) ⌋ style.

E DUR (*German*)· E major.

EGLISE (*French*). Church; as, *musique d'église*, ch music.

EGUALE (*Italian*).)
EGUALIANZA, con (*Italian*). } Equably; smoothly.
EGUALMENTE (*Italian*).

EIGHTH-NOTE. A quaver (♪).

EINFACH (*German*). Simple.

EINGANG (*German*). An introduction.

EINHEIT (*German*). Unity.

EINLEITUNG (*German*). An introduction.

EINLEITUNGSSATZ (*German*). An introductory move-ment.

EINSCHNITT (*German*). A phrase or imperfect musica sentence.

EIS (*German*). E sharp.

EISTEDDVOD (*Welsh*). An assemblage of bards.

ELEGANTEMENTE (*Italian*).
ELEGANTE (*Italian*). } With elegance, gracefully
ELEGANZA, con (*Italian*).

ELÈVE (*French*). A pupil.

EMBOUCHURE (*French*). The mouth-piece of a flute, hautboy, or other wind instrument.

E MOLL (*German*.) E minor.

EMPFINDUNG (*German*). Emotion, passion.

EMPHASIS. A particular stress or marked accent on any note, generally indicated by ➤, ∧, or *sf.*

ENCORE (*French*). An expression employed by the au-dience at theatres and concerts, to signify their desire that a song or other composition, should be repeated.

ENERGICAMENTE (*Italian*).
ENERGIA, con (*Italian*). } With energy.
ENERGICO (*Italian*).

ENFLER (*French*). To increase the tone.

ENGE (*German*). Close, condensed.

ENHARMONIC. One of the ancient genera; a scale which proceeds by quarter tones.

ENHARMONIQUE (*French*). Enharmonic.

ENSEIGNEMENT (*French*). Instruction.

ENSEIGNER (*French*). To instruct.

ENSEMBLE (*French*). A term applied to music in parts, when the several performers appear to be so animated by one and the same feeling, that the whole is given with that perfect smoothnss, both as regards time and style, as to leave nothing farther to be desired.

ENTR' ACTE (*French*). Music played between the acts of the drama.

ENTRATA (*Italian*). An introduction.

ENTUSIASMO, con (*Italian*). With enthusiasm.

ENTWURF (*German*). Sketch or rough draught of a composition.

EOLIAN. The name of one of the ancient modes.

EPICEDIUM (*Greek*). A funeral song, or dirge.

EPINETTE (*French*). A spinet, an old keyed instrument.

EPISODE. A portion of a composition not founded on the principal subject.

EPITHALAMIUM (*Greek*). A nuptial song, or ode.

E POI (*Italian*). *And then;* as, *e poi la coda,* and then the coda.

EQUAL VOICES. Compositions for *equal voices* are those in which either all male or all female voices are employed.

EQUISONANT. Of the same or like sound: a unison This term is often used in guitar playing, to express the different ways of stopping the same note.

EQUIVOCAL. A term applied to such chords as, by a mere change in the notation, may belong to several keys.

ERHÖHUNG (*German*). The raising the pitch of a note by a sharp.

ERNIEDRIGUNG (*German*). The depression of a note by means of a flat.

EROTIC. Amatory.

ERWEITERT (*German*). Expanded, extended.

ES (*German*). E flat.

ESSAI (*French*). An essay.

ESATTA (*Italian*). Exact.

ES DUR (*German*). E flat major.

ESECUZIONE (*Italian*). Execution.

ESEGUIRE (*Italian*). To execute or perform either vocally or on an instrument.

ESERCIZJ (*Italian plural*). Exercises, whether vocal or instrumental.

ESES (*German*). E double flat.

ES MOLL (*German*). E flat minor.

ESPACE (*French*). A space of the stave.

ESPAGNUOLO, all' (*Italian*). In the Spanish style.

ESPRESSIVO (*Italian*).
ESPRESSIONE, con (*Italian*). } With expression.

ESSEMPIO (*Italian*). An example.

ESSENTIAL NOTES. The notes forming any chord.

ESTINGUENDO (*Italian*). } Becoming extinct, dying away
ESTINTO (*Italian*). } in regard to time and tone.

ESTRAVAGANZA (*Italian*). Extravagant and wild, as to composition and performance.

ESTREMAMENTE (*Italian*). Extremely.

ESTRIBILHO. A favourite Portuguese song in 𝄕 time.

ET (*Latin*). And.

ET INCARNATUS EST (*Latin*). A portion of the Credo.

ETOUFFE (*French*). Stifled, damped, in harp playing.

ET RESURREXIT (*Latin*). Part of the Credo.

ETUDE (*French*). A study.

ET VITAM (*Latin*). A part of the Credo.

EUPHONY. Sweetness.

EVOLUTIO (*Latin*). Inversion.

EXECUTER (*French*). To execute or perform either vocally or on an instrument.

EXPRESSION. A performer is said to play *with expression* when he carefully observes the various modifications of *forte* and *piano*, *legato* and *staccato*, &c. and when, in addition to the above, he imparts to the composition which he is performing a particular charm arising from the impulse of his own feelings.

EXTEMPORE (*Latin*). Unpremeditated, extemporaneous.

EXTEMPORIZE. To perform unpremeditatedly.

EXTENDED HARMONY. See DISPERSED HARMONY.

EXTRANEOUS. Foreign, far-fetched.

EXTRANEOUS MODULATION. A modulation into some other than the original key and its relatives.

EXTREME. A term relating to intervals in an augmented state. By some authors it is used in conjunction with the word *sharp* or *flat ;* extreme sharp answering to *augmented*, and extreme flat to *diminished*.

F.

FA. A syllable applied, in solfaing, to the note F.

FA-BURDEN.
FALSO BORDONE (*Italian*).
FAUX BOURDON (*French*). } A term applied to several ancient species of counterpoint. With regard to modern times, it usually signifies a succession of chords of the sixth, where the interval of the sixth is formed by the extreme parts, and that of the third by the inner part.

FACILITA *(Italian)*. A facilitation, an easier adaption.

FACILMENTE *(Italian)*. Easily, with facility.

FAGOTTISTA *(Italian)*. A performer on the bassoon.

FAGOTTO *(Italian)*. A bassoon.

FAGOTTONE *(Italian)*. A double bassoon.

FA LA. The refrain or burden of many old songs.

FALSE CADENCE. A cadence in which the triad on the dominant is followed by that on the submediant or sixth degree of the scale.

FALSE FIFTH. An imperfect or diminished fifth: as, C sharp—G.

FALSE RELATION. That progression where a note which has occurred in one chord is found chromatically altered in a different part in the following chord.

FALSETTO *(Italian)*. Certain notes of a man's voice which are above its natural compass, and which can only be produced artificially.

FANDANGO. An expressive Spanish dance in $\frac{3}{4}$ time, generally accompanied with castanets.

FANFARE *(French)*. A trumpet tune.

FANTAISIE *(French)*. } A species of composition in which
FANTASIA *(Italian)*. } the author gives free scope to his ideas, without regard to those systematic and symmetrical forms which regulate other compositions.

FANTASTICAMENTE *(Italian)*. In a fantastic style.

FANTASTICO *(Italian)*. } Fantastic.
FANTASTIQUE *(French)*. }

FARANDOULE. The name of a lively French dance in $\frac{6}{8}$ time.

FARSA IN MUSICA *(Italian)*. A kind of little comic opera in one act.

FASCIE *(Italian plural)*. The sides or hoops of a violin tenor, &c.

FASTOSO (*Italian,*. With a lofty and splendid style of execution.

F DUR (*German*). The key of F major.

FERMO (*Italian*). Firm, resolute.

FERMATA (*Italian*). A pause.

FERMAMENTE (*Italian*). } With firmness and decision.
FERMATO (*Italian*).

FEROCE (*Italian*). } Fiercely, with an expression of
FEROCITÀ, con (*Italian*). } ferocity.

FES (*German*). F flat.

FIACCO (*Italian*). Weak, feeble.

FIASCO (*Italian*). A failure.

FIATO (*Italian*). The breath.

FIDICINAL. Of the violin species.

FIERAMENTE (*Italian*). } In a bold and energetic manner,
FIERO (*Italian*). } with vehemence.

FIFRE (*French*). A fife.

FIFTEENTH. An organ-stop, tuned two octaves above the Diapasons; also an interval of two octaves.

FIGURATO (*Italian*). } Figured; as *Basso figurato,* a
FIGURÉ (*French*). } figured bass.

FIGURED BASS. A bass having figures placed over the notes to indicate the harmony.

FILAR LA VOCE (*Italian*). To gradually augment and diminish the sound of the voice.

FINALE. The last piece of any act of an opera, or of a concert; or the last movement of a symphony or sonata, in the German style.

FIN (*French*). } The end. This expression is generally used
FINE (*Italian*). } to indicate the termination of a musical composition.

FINGERSATZ (*German*). Fingering.

FINITO (*Italian*). Concluded. terminated.

FIN QUI (*Italian*). To this place.

FINTO (*Italian*). Feigned, interrupted, in regard to cadences, &c.

FIORITURE (*Italian.*) Embellishments in singing; divisions of rapid notes.

FIS (*German*). F sharp.

FIS DUR (*German*). The key of F sharp major.

FISFIS (*German*). F double sharp.

FIS MOLL (*German*). The key of F sharp minor.

FISTULA (*Latin*). A pipe, or flute in general.

FITHELE. The ancient name of the fiddle.

FLAUTANDO (*Italian*). } With a flute-like tone. This term
FLAUTATO (*Italian*). } is sometimes met with in violin music, and the desired quality of tone is obtained by drawing the bow smoothly and gently across the strings, over that end of the finger-board nearest the bridge.

FLAUTINO (*Italian*). An octave flute.

FLAUTISTA (*Italian*). A performer on the flute.

FLAUTO (*Italian*). A flute.

FLAUTO PICCOLO (*Italian*). An octave flute, or a flageolet.

FLAUTO TRAVERSO (*Italian*). The German flute.

FLEBILE (*Italian*). } In a mournful style.
FLEBILMENTE (*Italian*). }

FLESSIBILITÀ, con (*Italian*). With flexibility.

F-LÖCHER (*German plur*). The sound-holes of a violin, tenor, &c.

FLON-FLON. The burden of certain old vaudevilles. The term is now applied in contempt to any air resembling them in style.

FLORID. Ornamental, figured, embellished.

FLÜGEL (*German*). A harpsichord.

FLUTE-A-BEC (*French*). An English flute

FLUTE ALLEMANDE (*French*). } The German flute.
————— **TRAVERSIERE** (*French*) }

F MOLL (*German*). The key of F minor.

FOCOSO (*Italian*). With fire.

FOLLIA (*Spanish*). A Spanish air, or dance-tune. so called.

FORTE (*Italian*). } Loud.
FOR. (*abbrev.*) }

FORLANA (*Italian*). } A lively Venetian dance in $\frac{6}{8}$ time.
FORLANE (*French*). }

FORTEMENT (*French*). Loudly, with force.

FORTE-PIANO (*Italian*). The piano is so called by reason of its capability of modifying the intensity of the sounds.

FORTISSIMO (*Italian*). Very loud.

FORTSETZUNG (*German*). A continuation.

FORZANDO (*Italian*). } This term implies that the note is to
FORZ. (*abbrev.*) } be marked with particular emphasis or force.

FORZA (*Italian*). } Force; as, *con forza*, with force, ve-
FORZATO (*Italian*). } hemently.

FRANCHEZZA, con (*Italian*). With freedom; boldly.

FRASI (*Italian plu*). Phrases, short musical sentences.

FREDDAMENTE (*Italian*). } Coldly, with coldness.
FREDDEZZA, con (*Italian*). }

FREDON (*French*). A flourish, or other extemporaneous embellishment.

FRENCH SIXTH. The name of a chord composed of a major third, extreme fourth, and extreme sixth; as

F ♯
D
C
A ♭

FRETS. Small projecting divisons placed across the finger-boards of guitars, lutes, &c., to indicate where the notes are to be stopped.

FRETTA, con (*Italian*). Increasing the time.

FREY (*German*). Free; as *freye Schreibart*, the free style of composition.

FROSCH (*German*) The nut of a bow for the violin, tenor bass, &c.

F SCHLÜSSEL (*German*). The F clef.

FUGA (*Italian*). A fugue.

FUGA DOPPIA (*Italian*). A double fugue, or fugue on two subjects.

FUGATO (*Italian*). In the fugue or strict style

FUGHETTA (*Italian*). A short fugue.

FUGUE. A composition in the strict style, in which a subject being proposed by one part, is repeated and imitated by the other parts in succession and according to certain laws.*

FUGUE RENVERSÉE (*French*). A fugue, the answer of which is made in contrary motion to that of the subject.

FÜHRER (*German*). The subject of a fugue.

FULL. For all the voices or instruments. In cathedral music it implies that the passage is to be sung by both sides of the choir.

FULL ANTHEM. An anthem in four or more parts, without verses, to be sung in chorus.

FULL SCORE. A score containing the whole of the vocal and instrumental parts of a composition.

FULL SERVICE. A service without any verse parts

---

* See Hamilton's Catechism on Fugue, as also Albrechtsberger's and Cherubini's Treatises on Composition.

FUNDAMEN1AL BASS. A bass formed of the roots of chords only. A bass of this sort is not meant to be played, but merely to serve as a test of the correct progression of the harmony.

FUNEBRE (*French* and *Italian*). } Funeral; as, *marche*
FUNEREO (*Italian*).   }   *funèbre,* a funeral march.

FUNZIONI (*Italian plu.*) Sacred musical performances in general, as oratorios, masses, &c.

FUOCO, con (*Italian*). With fire, with intense animation.

FURIA, con (*Italian*).   ⎫
FURIBONDO (*Italian*).   ⎬ With extreme vehemence;
FURIOSAMENTE (*Italian*). ⎬   furiously.
FURIOSO (*Italian*).   ⎭

FURLANO (*Italian*). An antiquated dance.

FURNITURE. An organ-stop, consisting of several ranks of pipes.

FURORE, con (*Italian*). With fury, with great agitation.

FUSA (*Latin*). A quaver.

FUSELLA (*Latin*). The name formerly applied to the demi-semiquaver.

G.

GAIAMENT (*Italian*).   } In a cheerful and lively style.
GAIEMENTE (*French*). }

GAI (*French*).   ⎫
GAIO (*Italian*).   ⎬ Gaily, cheerfully.
GAJO (*Italian*).   ⎭

GAGLIARDA (*Italian*). ⎫
GAILLARDE (*French*). ⎬ A lively dance-tune, in triple time.
GALLIARD.   ⎭

GALANTEMENTE (*Italian*). Gallantly, boldly.

GALOPADE (*French*). A galop, a quick German dance tune.

GALOP (*German*). } A quick species of dance, generally
GALOPPE (*French.*) } in $\frac{2}{4}$ time.

GAMME (*French*). The scale of any key.

GAMUT. The scale of notes belonging to any key.

GANZE (*German*). Whole: as, *ganze note*, a whole note or semibreve; *ganze ton*, a whole tone.

GARBO, con (*Italian*). With simplicity, without pretension affectedly.

GARRIRE (*Italian*). To warble like a bird.

GAUCHE (*French.*) Left; as *main gauche*, left hand.

GAVOT. A lively dance in common time.

GAVOTTA (*Italian*). A gavot, a lively species of dance

G DUR (*German*). The key of G major.

GEBROCHENE AKKORDE (*German plural*). Broken chords; arpeggios.

GEBUNDEN (*German*). Connected, syncopated, in regard to the style of playing or writing.

GEDACHT (*German*). Stopped, in opposition to the open pipes in an organ.

GEFÄHRTE (*German*). The answer of a fugue.

GEFÜHL, mit (*German*). With feeling and sentiment.

GEGENBEWEGUNG (*German*). Contrary motion.

GEHEND (*German*). This word signifies a degree of movement similar to that implied by *Andante*.

GEIGE (*German*). The violin.

GENERA (*Latin plu.*) } The different modes of dividing the
GENUS (*Latin*). } octave, as by tones and semitones conjointly; by semitones only; and, theoretically, by quarter-tones only. The first is called the diatonic or natural genus; the second, the chromatic or artificial genus; and the last, the enharmonic genus.

GENERALBASS (German). Thorough-bass.

GENEROSO (Italian). Nobly; in a dignified manner.

GENRE (French). Style. Also genus; as,

GENRE CHROMATIQUE (French). The chromatic genus.

GENTILEZZA, con (Italian). With grace and elegance.

GERADE BEWEGUNG (German). Similar motion.

GERADE TAKTART (German). Common time.

GERMAN SIXTH. The name applied by some writers to a chord composed of a major third, perfect fifth, and extreme sixth; as,

$$
\begin{array}{l}
\text{A} \sharp \\
\text{G} \\
\text{E} \\
\text{C}
\end{array}
$$

GES (German). G flat.

GESANG (German). Singing, or the art of singing; also a song.

GESCHWIND (German). Quick; as,

GESCHWIND MARSCH (German). A quick march.

GES DUR (German). The key of G flat major.

GIGA (Italian).
GIGUE (French). } A jig, or lively species of dance.

GIOCOSAMENTE (Italian).
GIOCOSO (Italian). } Humorousiy, with sportiveness.

GIOJOSO (Italian). Joyously; with buoyant hilarity.

GIOVALE (Italian). Jovially.

GIS (German). G sharp.

GIS MOLL (German). The key of G sharp minor.

GIUOCO (Italian). A stop of an organ.

GIUSTAMENTE (Italian). Justly; with precision.

GIUSTO (Italian). In just and exact time.

GLEE. A composition for three or more voices, generally in a cheerful style.*

---

* See Horsley's or Clementi's Collections for fine specimens.

GLI (*Italian plu.*) The; as, *gli stromenti*, the instruments.

GLISSANDO (*Italian*). In a gliding manner.

GLISSICATO (*Italian*) In a gentle and gliding manner.

GLISSER (*French*). To glide along the key-board by turning the nails towards the edges of the keys.

GLORIA (*Latin*) A principal movement of the mass or catholic service.

G MOLL (*German*). The key cf G minor.

GONG. An Indian pulsatile instrument, consisting of a large circular plate of bell-metal.

GORGHEGGI (*Italian plu.*) Rapid divisions, as exercise. for the voice in singing.

GRACES. Occasional embellishments, sometimes indica... by the composer, sometimes spontaneously introduced by the performer. The most important of these are the *appoggiatura*, the *turn*, and the *shake*.*

GRADAZIONE, con (*Italian*). With gradation; gradually.

GRADO (*Italian*). A degree. *Di grado* implies that a melody moves by degrees ascending and descending, and not *di salto*, by skips of larger intervals.

GRADUALE (*Latin*). Part of the Catholic service, sung between the Epistle and Gospel.

GRADUELLEMENT (*French*). Gradually, by degrees.

GRADUAL MODULATION. Modulation in which, before the modulating chord, some chord is taken which may he considered as belonging either to the key we are in, or that to which we are going.

GRAN (*Italian*).
GRANDE (*Italian*). } Great; grand.

GRANDIOSO (*Italian*).
GRAN GUSTO (*Italian*). } In a grand and elevated style.

---

* See Hamilton's Musical Grammar.

GRAND MESURE A DEUX TEMS (*French*). C time.

GRAPPA (*Italian*). The brace or character serving to con-nect two or more staves.

GRATIAS AGIMUS (*Latin*). Part of the Gloria.

GRAVEMENTE (*Italian*). With gravity; dignified and solemn.

GRAVE (*Italian*). A very slow and solemn movement; also a deep, low pitch in the scale of sounds.

GRAVITA, con (*Italian*). With gravity.

GRAZIA, con (*Italian*).
GRAZIOSAMENTE (*Italian*). } In a flowing and graceful
GRAZIOSO (*Italian*). style.

GREAT ORGAN. In an organ with three rows of keys this is usually the middle row; it is so called from contain-ing the greatest number of stops, as also from the pipes being voiced louder than those in the *swell* or the *choir organ*.

GREGORIANISCHE GESANG (*German*). The Grego-rian chant.

GREGORIAN MUSIC. Sacred compositions introduced into the Catholic service by Pope Gregory.

GREGORIAN TONES. This term sometimes refers to the Chants used for the Psalms in the Roman Catholic service, and at others to the ancient *modes* or *tones* on which those chants are based. (See CHURCH MODES).

GRIFFBRET (*German*). The finger-board of a violin, violoncello, &c.

GROS-FA. The name formerly applied to old church music in square notes, semibreves, and minims.

GROSSE (*German*). Major, in regard to intervals.

GROSSE CAISSE (*French*). The great drum.

GROSSE SONATE (*German plur.*) Grand sonatas.

GROSSO (*Italian*). Great, grand, full. as oncerto grosso, a concert for many instruments.

GROS TAMBOUR (*French*). The great drum.

GROUND. A bass, consisting of a few simple notes, intended as a theme on which, at each repetition, a new melody is constructed.

GROUP. An assemblage of several short notes tied together.

GRUNDSTIMME (*German*). The bass.

GRUNDTON (*German*). The bass note.

GRUPPETTO (*Italian*). A group of notes ; a *turn*

GRUPPO (*Italian*). A turn, or grace.

G SCHLÜSSEL (*German*). The C clef.

GUARACHA. A Spanish dance.

GUDDOK. The name of a rustic violin with three strings used among the Russian peasantry.

GUERRIERO (*Italian*). In a martial and warlike style.

GUIDA (*Italian*). A guide: as *guida armonica*, a guide to harmony.

GUIDA (*Italian*).
GUIDON (*French*). } The character called a *direct*.

GUIDONIAN SYLLABLES. See ARETINIAN SYLLABLES.

GUSTO, *con*, (*Italian*).
GUSTOSO } With taste, elegantly.

GUTTURAL. Formed too much in the throat.

H.

H. This letter is used by the Germans for B natural

HACKBRETT (*German*.) The dulcimer.

HALBTON (*German*). A semitone.

HALBCADENZ (*German*). A half cadence, a cadence the dominant.

HALBNOTE (*German*). } A minim (♩).
HALF-NOTE

HALLELUJAH. A Hebrew word signifying "Praise the Lord."

HALS (*German*). The neck of a violin, tenor, &c.

HAND-GUIDE.* An instrument invented by Kalkbrenner, to insure a good position of the hands and arms on the piano-forte.

HARDIMENT (*French*). With boldness and animation.

HARFE (*German*). A harp.

HARMONIPHON. A little instrument, with a keyboard like a pianoforte, invented in 1837, and intended to supply the place of the hautboys in the orchestra. The sounds are pro-duced from small metal tongues, acted upon by blowing through a flexible tube.

HARMONICA. A musical instrument, the tones of which are produced from globular glasses.

HARMONICI (*Italian plural*). Harmonics in violin music.

HARMONIE (*French and German.*). Harmony in general, also music expressly composed for a military band.

HARMONICS. Certain indistinct sounds which, by atten-tively listening to the vibrations of any deep-toned musical string, may be heard to accompany the principal sound. *Harmonics* are also certain artificial notes produced from the violin, violoncello, harp, &c., and which somewhat resemble the tones of a flageolet.

HARMONIST. One acquainted with the laws of harmony

---

* This ingenious and useful instrument may be had of Messrs. Cocks
e manufacturers.

HARMONY. The art of combining several sounds, so as to form chords, and of treating the combinations thus formed.*

HARPSICHORD. An instrument much used before the invention of the pianoforte: its strings were of wire, and it was furnished with one and sometimes with two rows of keys.

HART (*German*). Major, in regard to keys and modes.

HAUPT (*German*). Principal; as,

HAUPTMANUAL (*German*). The set of keys belonging to the great organ.

HAUPTNOTE (*German*). ⎫ The principal note of a shake, or
HAUPT-TON (*German*). ⎬ that over which the mark *tr* is
⎭ placed.

HAUPTPERIOD (*German*). A capital period.

HAUPTSATZ (*German*). The principal subject or theme.

HAUPTSCHLUSS (*German.*) A final cadence.

HAUPTSTIMME (*German*). A principal part.

HAUPTWERK (*German*). The great organ.

HAUSSE (*French*). The nut of a violin or other bow.

HAUSSER (*French*). To raise or sharpen the pitch.

HAUT (*French*). Acute, high, shrill: as,

HAUT CONTRE (*French*). High, or counter tenor.

—— DESSUS (*French*). First treble.

H DUR (*German*). B major.

HEMIDIAPENTE (*Greek*). The diminished or imperfect fifth.

HEPTACHORD. A scale or system of seven notes

HERABSTRICH (*German*). ⎫ A down-bow
HERSTRICH (*German*). ⎬

* See Hamilton's Catechism of Harmony and Thorough Bass

G 2

HEXACHORD. A scale or system of six notes.

HIDDEN CONSECUTIVES. Such as occur in passing, by similar motion, from an imperfect to a perfect concord, or from one perfect concord to another of a different kind.

HINAUFSTRICH (*German*). } An up-bow.
HINSTRICH (*German*).

HIS (*German*). B sharp.

H MOLL (*German*). The key of B minor.

HOCHZEITMARSCH (*German*). A nuptial march.

HOMOPHONY. In unison.

HOPSWALZER (*German*). Quick waltzes.

HORNPIPE. The name of an old dance in triple time Modern tunes of this name are usually in common time.

HOSANNA (*Latin*). Part of the Sanctus.

HÜLFSNOTE (*German*). } The auxiliary note of a shake.
HÜLFSTON (*German*).

HURTIG (*German*). *Quick.* Implying a degree of movement similar to that indicated by the word *Allegro.*

HYPER (*Greek*). Above.

HYPO (*Greek*). Below.

I.

IAMBUS. A musical foot, consisting of one short and one long note.

IASTIAN: The name of one of the ancient modes.

IL (*Italian*). The ; as, *il violino*, the violin.

IL PIU (*Italian*). The most.

  MBOCCATURA (*Italian*). The mouth piece of a wind-instrument.

IMITANDO (*Italian*). Imitating ; as, *imitando la voce*, imitating the inflections of the voice.

IMITAZIONE (*Italian*). An imitation.

IMPAZIENTEMENTE (*Italian*). Impatiently.

IMPERFECT. Less than perfect in respect to intervals and chords.

IMPERFECT CADENCE. A cadence in which the triad on the tonic or key-note is followed by that on the dominant.

IMPERFECT CONSONANCES. The major and minor third, and the major and minor sixth.

IMPETO, *con* (*Italian*).

IMPETUOSAMENTE (*Italian*). ⎫ With impetuosity; impe-
IMPETUOSITÀ, *con* (*Italian*). ⎬ tuously.
IMPETUOSO (*Italian*). ⎭

IMPONENTE (*Italian*). Imposingly, haughtily.

IMPRESSARIO (*Italian*). The conductor or manager of an opera or concert.

IMPROMPTU (*French*). An extemporaneous production.

IMPROVVISAMENTE (*Italian*). Extemporaneously.

IMPROVVISARE (*Italian*). To compose or sing extemporaneously.

IMPROVVISATORI (*Italian plur*). Persons gifted witt the power of reciting or singing verses extemporaneously.

IN (*Italian*). In: as, *in tempo*, in time.

IN ALT (*Italian*). Notes are said to be *in alt* when situated above the F on the fifth line of the treble stave.

IN ALTISSIMO (*Italian*). An epithet applied to those notes which are situated above the F over the third additional or ledger line in the treble.

INCISORE DI NOTE (*Italian*). An engraver of music.

INCORDARE (*Italian*). To string an instrument.

INDECISO (*Italian*). In an undecided manner.

INDIFFERENZA, *con* (*Italian*). With indifference

INFANTILE *Italian*). Child-like; infantine; the thin quality of tone observable in the upper notes of some female voices.

INFERNALE (*Italian*). Infernal.

INFLATILE. Wind instruments, as flutes, clarionets, &c. are so termed.

INFLECTION. Any change or modification in the pitch or tone of the voice.

INGANNO (*Italian*). A deception. It is generally applied to interrupted cadences, though occasionally also to any unusual resolution of a discord, or unexpected modulation.

INNOCENTEMENTE (*Italian*).
INNOCENTE (*Italian*). } In an artless and simple style.
INNOCENZA, con (*Italian*).

INQUIETO (*Italian*). Perturbed, uneasy, with disquietude

INSEGNAMENTO (*Italian*). Instruction.

INSENSIBILMENTE (*Italian*). Insensibly; by small degrees.

INSTRUMENT À ARCHET (*French*). A bow instrument.

INSTRUMENT À VENT (*French*). A wind instrument.

INTERLUDE. } An intermediate strain or move-
INTERLUDIUM (*Latin*). } ment.

INTERMEZZI (*Italian plural.*) Interludes or detached dances introduced between the acts of an opera.

INTERMEZZO (*Italian*). Intermediate, placed between two others.

INTERRUZIONE (*Italian*). An interruption: as, *senza interruzione*, play on without interruption.

INTERVAL. The distance, or difference of pitch, between two notes.

INTERVALLE (*French*). } An interval
INTERVALLO (*Italian*).

INTONATION. } The act of producing or emit-
INTONAZIONE (*Italian*). } ting musical sounds, particularly in singing.

INTRADA (*Italian*). } A short introductory move-
INTRODUZIONE (*Italian*). } ment.

INTREPIDAMENTE (*Italian*). } With intrepidity.
INTREPIDEZZA, con (*Italian*). }

INTRODUCIMENTO (*Italian*). An introduction.

INTROITUS (*Latin*). The commencement of the mass or
Catholic divine service.

INVERSION. A change of position with regard to intervals and chords; so that the upper notes are placed below,
and the lower notes above, &c.

INVITATORIUM (*Latin*). In the Roman Catholic Church
this is the name given to the antiphone or response to the
Psalm, "*Venite exultemus.*"

INVOCAZIONE (*Italian*). A prayer or invocation.

IONIAN. See IASTIAN.

IRATAMENTE (*Italian*). } Angrily
IRATO (*Italian*). }

IRLANDAIS (*French*). } An air or dance-tune in the
IRLANDAISE (*French*). } Irish style.

IRONICAMENTE (*Italian*). Ironically.

IRRESOLUTO (*Italian*). Irresolutely, hesitatingly, dubi-
ously.

ISTESSO (*Italiun*). The same; as, *istesso tempo*, the same
time.

ISTRUMENTAZIONE (*Italian*). Instrumentation.

ITALIAN SIXTH. The name given by some authors to a
chord composed of a major third and augmented sixth; as,

D ♯
A
♭

ITALIENNE, *a l'* (*French*).   In the Italian style.

ITE, MISSA EST (*Latin*).   The termination of the mass, sung by the priest to Gregorian music.

J.

JAEGER CHOR (*German*).   Hunting chorus.

JEUX (*French plural*).   Stops in organ playing; as, *jeux forts*, loud stops; *grand jeu*, full organ.

JIG.   A brisk and lively air.

JONGLEURS (*French plural*).   Itinerant musicians were formerly so called.

JUSTE (*French*).   Perfect with regard to intervals.

JUSTESSE (*French*).   Exactness or purity of intonation.

K.

KALAMAIKA.   A lively Hungarian dance in $\frac{2}{4}$ time.

KAMMER (*German*).   Chamber; as,

KAMMER-CONCERT.   A chamber concert.

———— MUSIK.   Chamber-music.

KAPELLMEISTER (*German*).   A chapel-master.

KECKHEIT (*German*).   Boldness; as, *mit Keckheit vorge-tragen*, with a bold and vigorous style of performance.

KEMAN.   A Turkish violin with three strings.

KEY.   The lever by which the notes of a pianoforte or organ are made to sound.   Flutes, hautboys, and other wind-instruments, have also their keys, by which certain holes are opened or shut.   A key is also an assemblage of notes, each of which has a fixed and distinct relation to one particular note, which for this reason, is called the key-note.*

-----

* See Forde on the Key in Music.

KEYBOARD. The row of keys of a pianoforte or organ when spoken of collectively, is so termed.

KEY-NOTE. A note to which a series of other subordinate notes bear a distinct relation.

KIRCHEN-MUSIK (*German*). Church music.

KIT. A small or pocket violin, used by dancing-masters.

KLANG (*German*). Sound.

KLANGESCHLECHT (*German*). A genus: as, *chromatisches klangeschlecht*, the chromatic genus.

KLAPPE (*German*). A key belonging to any wind instrustrument.

KLAPPEN FLUGELHORN (*German*). The keyed bugle.

KLAPPTROMPETE (*German*). A keyed trumpet.

KLEIN (*German*). Minor, in regard to intervals.

KREUZ (*German*). The character called a *sharp*.

KURZ (*German*). Short.

KYRIE (*Greek*). Lord. In the Catholic service, the first movement of the mass begins with music set to the words *Kyrie eleison, Christe eleison*, Lord have mercy upon us, Christ have mercy upon us.

L.

L.
L. H. } Indicates the left hand in pianoforte music.

LA. A syllable applied in solfaing to the note A.

LA (*Italian* and *French*). The; as, *la voce*, the voice.

LA CHASSE (*French*). A piece of music in the hunting style.

LACRIMOSO (*Italian*).
LAGRIMOSO (*Italian*). } In a mournful, dolorous style.

L'AME (*French*) The sound-post of a violin, tenor, &c.

LAMENTABILE (*Italian*).
LAMENTABILMENTE (*Italian*)
LAMENTANDO (*Italian*).
LAMENTEVOLMENTE (*Italian*).
AMENTIVOLE (*Italian*).
AMENTOSO (*Italian*).
} Plaintively, mournfully.

LÄNDLER (*German*). A country-dance or air in a rustic and popular style, generally in $\frac{3}{8}$ time.

LANDU. See LUNDU.

LANGSAM (*German*). Slowly.

LANGUEMENTE (*Italian*).
LANGUENDO (*Italian*).
} Languishingly.

LANGUENTE (*Italian*).
LANGUIDO (*Italian*).
} With languor.

LARGAMENTE (*Italian*).
LARGHEZZA (*Italian*).
} In a full, free, broad style of performance.

LARGE. The name of a note shaped thus ▬ found in ancient music. It is equal to eight semibreves.

LARGEMENT (*French*). Very slow.

LARGHETTO (*Italian*). Indicates a time slow and measured in its movement, but less so than *largo*.

LARGHISSIMO (*Italian*). Extremely slow.

LARGO (*Italian*). A very slow and solemn degree of movement.

LARIGOT (*French*). An organ-stop, tuned an octave above the twelfth.

LAUDAMUS (*Latin*). *We praise Thee.* A part of the mass.

LAUF (*German*). That part of a violin, tenor, &c., into which the pegs are inserted; also a rapid succession of notes.

LAUTE (*German*). The lute.

LE (*Italian plural*). The as, *le voci*, the voices.

LEADING NOTE. The seventh note of the scale of any key, when at the distance of a semitone below the key-note.

LEBHAFT (*German*). Lively.

LEÇON (*French*). A lesson or instructive composition for some instrument.

LEDGER LINES, or LEGER LINES. Those temporary lines which are occasional y drawn above or below the stave, in order to obtain additional situations for the heads of the notes.

LEGATISSIMO (*Italian*). Exceedingly smooth and connected.

LEGATO (*Italian*). In a smooth and connected manner.

LEGÉREMENT (*Erench*). With lightness and gaiet .

LEGGIARDO (*Italian*). Light, gentle.

LEGGIERAMENTE (*Italian*). Lightly, gently.

LEGGIEREZZA, con (*Italian*). } With lightness and facility
LEGGIERO (*Italian*). } of execution.

LEGGIERISSIMO (*Italian*). With the utmost lightness and facility.

LEGNO, col (*Italian*). With the bowstick.

LEICHT (*German*). Easy.

LENTANDO (*Italian*). With increasing slowness

LENTEMENT (*French*).
LENTEMENTE (*Italian*). } In slow time.
LENTO (*Italian*).

LENTEUR, avec (*French*). } With slowness, in a sedate and
LENTEZZA, con (*Italian*). } lingering ; pace.

LETTURA (*Italian*). Reading, as in the case of music.

LIAISON (*Erench*). Smoothness of connection ; also a bind or tie.

LIBERAMENTE (*Italian*). Freely, easily.

LIBRETTO (*Italian*). The book of the words of an Italian opera is so called.

LIÉ (*French*). Smoothly, connectedly. Synonymous with *legato*.

LIED (*German*). A song.

LIGATURE. The old name for a tie or bind.

LIGNE (*French*). ⎫
LINEA (*Italian*). ⎬ A line of the stave.
LINIE (*German*). ⎭

LINK (*German*). Left; as, *linke Hand*, the left hand.

LIRE (*French*). To read, as regards music.

L'ISTESSO MOVIMENTO (*Italian*). ⎫ In the same time
L'ISTESSO TEMPO (*Italian*). ⎬ as the previous movement.

LIUTO (*Italian*). The lute.

LOBGESANG (*German*). A hymn, a song of praise.

LOCO (*Latin*). This words implies that a passage is to be played just as it is written in regard to pitch: it generally occurs after 8*va alta*, or 8*va bassa*.

LONG. The name of a note formerly in use, equal to four semibreves.

LOURE (*French*). An old-fashioned French dance.

LUGUBRE (*Italian*). Mournfully, sadly.

LUNDU. A Portuguese dance in $\frac{2}{4}$ or $\frac{2}{2}$ time.

LUNGA PAUSA (*Italian*). An expression signifying that the performer must cease playing for a considerable time.

LUSINGANDO (*Italian*).
LUSINGATO (*Italian*).
LUSINGHEVOLE (*Italian*). ⎬ Soothingly, persua-
LUSINGHEVOLMENTE (*Italian*). sively
LUSINGHIERO (*Italian*)
LUSINGHIERE (*Italian*).

LUTE. A stringed instrument, formerly much esteemed.

LYDIAN. The name of one of the ancient modes.

LYRA (*Italian*). The lyre, a well-known musical instrument.

LYRIC. Poetry adapted for and intended to be set to music.

M.

MA (*Italian*). But; as, *allegro ma non troppo*, quick, but not too much so.

MADRIGAL. } An elaborate composition for
MADRIGALE (*Italian*). } voices in five or six parts, in the ancient style of imitation and fugue.

MAESTA, con (*Italian*). } With majestic and dignified expres-
MAESTOSO (*Italian*). } sion.

MAESTRO DEL CORO (*Italian*). The master of the choir.

MAESTRO DI CAPELLA (*Italian*). Chapel-master, or director of the chapel music in the Catholic service.

MAGGIORE (*Italian*). } Major, greater,—in opposition to
MAJEUR (*French*). } minor, less,—in respect to scales, intervals, modes, &c.

MAGNIFICAT. A canticle, sung by the Virgin in the house of Zachariah. A part of the Vespers in the Catholic evening service.

MAIN (*French.*) The hand; as,

——— DROITE (*French*). The right hand.

——— GAUCHE (*French*). The left hand.

MAITRE DE CHAPELLE (*French*). Chapel-master.

MAJOR. Greater, in respect to intervals and modes.

MAJOR MODE. One of the two modern modes; that is which the third from the key-note is major.

MALINCONIA (*Italian*).
MALINCONICAMENTE (*Italian* } In a melanch.... style.
MALINCONICO (*Italian*).

MANCANDO (*Italian*). Indicates a aqual decrease u. th quantity of tone.

MANCHE (*French*). The neck of a violin.

MANDOLINE (*French*). } An instrument wit four acrings,
MANDOLINO (*Italian*). } and with frets, like guitar · ¹ is tuned like the violin.

MANICO (*Italian*). The neck of a violin, tenor, &

MANIEREN (*German plural*). Graces, embellishments.

MANO (*Italian*). The hand; as,

——— DRITTA (*Italian*). The right hand.

——— SINISTRA (*Italian*). The left hand.

MANUAL (*German*). The key-board.

MARCATO (*Italian*). In a marked and emphatic styl

MARCATISSIMO (*Italian*). Very strongly marked.

MARCHE (*French*). In harmony, a symmetrical sequ of chords.

MARCHE (*French*). }
MARCIA (*Italian*). } A march.
MARSCH (*German*). }

MARTELLANDO (*Italian*). Strongly marking, c: as it were, hammering the notes.

MARTELLARE (*Italian*). To strike the notes so as to imitate the blow of a hammer.

MARTELLATO (*Italian*). Forcibly marked; hammered.

MARZIALE (*Italian*). In a martial style.

MASK. } A sort of musical drama or operetta performed
MASQUE. } by characters in masks.

MASS. A Catholic musical service, consisting of several movements.

MÄSSIG (*German*). Moder....., *massig langsam*, moderately slow.

MASURE (*German*).
MASURECK (*German*).
MASURKA (*German*).
MAZOURK (*German.*)
MAZURECK (*German*).
MAZURKA (*German*).
} A quick Polish dance, in $\frac{3}{8}$ time, with a peculiar rhythmic construction, somewhat like tnat of the polacca.

MATINS. The early morning service of the Catholic Church.

MAXIMA. See LARGE.

MEAN. The name formerly given to the *tenor part* of a composition.

MEDESIMO (*Italian*). The same; as,

MEDESIMO TEMPO (*Italian*). In the same time.

MEDIANT.
MEDIANTE (*French*).
} The mediant or third note of the scale.

MELANGE (*French*). A composition founded on sever_ favourite airs; a medley.

MELODIA (*Italian*).
MELODIE (*French*).
} Meloay.

MELODIOSA (*Italian*). Melodious.

MELODRAMA.
MELODRAME (*French*).
MELODRAMMA (*Italian*).
} A species of pantomim**i** drama, in which much o the interest depends u**m**' descriptive instrumental music.

MELODY. A well-ordered progression of single sounas.

MELOPŒIA (*Greek*). Melody.

MEME (*French*). The same; as,

MEME MOUVEMENT (*French*). In the same time

MEN (*Italian*).
MENO (*Italian*).
} Less; as,

MEN FORTE (*Italian*). Less loud.

MEN PRESTO (*Italian*). Less quick.

MEN PIANO (*Italian*). Somewhat softer

MENO VIVO (*Italian*). With less spirit.

MENUET (*French*). A minuet.

MESSA (*Italian*). A mass or Catholic musical service.

MESSA CONCERTATA (*Italian*). A concerted mass.

MESSA DI VOCE (*Italian*). A swelling and diminishing of the voice on a long holding note.*

MESSE (*French*). A mass, or Catholic musical service.

MESTO (*Italian*). Mournfully, sadly, pathetically.

MESTOSO (*Italian*). Sadly, pensively.

MESURE (*French*). The bar or measure.

MESURE À DEUX TEMS (*French*). Common time.

MESURE A TROIS TEMS (*French*). Triple time.

METALLICO (*Italian*). Of a metallic quality.

METHODE (*French*). A treatise or book of instructions.

METRONOME (*French*). An ingenious instrument for indicating the exact time of a musical piece, by means of a pendulum, which may be shortened or lengthened at pleasure.†

METRUM (*German*). The measure or time.

MEZZA BRAVURA (*Italian*). A song of moderate difficulty as to execution.

———— MANICA (*Italian*). The half-shift, 'n violin playing.

---

* For the importance of the Messa di Voce in the formation of the Voice, see Hamilton's Catechism on Singing.

† See Hamilton's Treatise on the Metronome and Handguide. . Bell Metronome, price 42s., and ditto without the bell are sold for the Proprietor by his agents, Messrs. Cocks

MEZZA VOCE (*Italian*). With moderation as to tone; rather soft than loud.

MEZZO (*Italian*). In a middling degree or manner; as,

———— CARATTERE (*Italian*). Implies a moderate degree of expression and execution.

———— FORTE (*Italian*). Rather loud.

———— PIANO (*Italian*). Rather soft.

———— SOPRANO (*Italian*). A female voice of a lower pitch than the soprano or treble. A C clef for this voice used to be placed on the second line of the stave.

MEZZO TUONO (*Italian*). A semitone.

MI (*Italian*). A syllable used in solfaing to designate E, or the third note of the major scale.

MI CONTRA FA (*Latin*). An expression signifying, among theorists, a false relation.

MILITARMENTE (*Italian*). In a military style.

MINACCIOSO (*Italian*). In a threatening style.

MINEUR (*French*). Minor in speaking of keys and intervals.

MINIM. A note of which the duration is equal to one-half the semibreve.

MINOR. Less in regard to intervals.

MINORE (*Italian*). Less in respect to intervals; minor as to modes and keys.

MINOR MODE. One of the two modern modes, in which the third from the key-note is minor.

MINSTRELS. A class of wandering poet-musicians of the eleventh and following centuries.

MINUETTO (*Italian*) A minuet; a slow dance in triple time.

MISERERE (*Latin*). *Have Mercy* A psalm of supplication.

MISSA (*Latin*). A mass. In a musical sense, the mass consists of five principal movements—the *Kyrie, Gloria, Credo, Sanctus,* and *Agnus Dei.*

MISSAL. An abridgment of the chants introduced into the Catholic service by Gregory the Great.

MISTERIOSAMENTE (*Italian*). } In a mysterious man-
MISTERIOSO (*Italian*). } ner.

MISURATO (*Italian*). In measured or strict time.

MIT (*German*). With; as, *mit begleitung,* with an accompaniment.

MITTELSTIMMEN (*German plural*). The middle parts.

MIXED CADENCE. The triad on the subdominant followed by that on the dominant.

MIXOLYDIAN. The name of one of the ancient modes.

MIXTURE. An organ-stop, consisting of two or more ranks of pipes.

MOCIGANGA (*Spanish*). A musical interlude common in Spain.

MODE. A certain arrangement of tones and semitones.

MODERATAMENTE (*Italian*).} With a moderate degree
MODERATO (*Italian*). } of quickness.
MODERAZIONE, con (*Italian*).}

MODERATISSIMO (*Italian*). In very moderate time.

MODESTO (*Italian*). Modestly, quietly.

MODINHA. A short Portuguese song.

MODO (*Italian*). A mode; as,

—— **MAGGIORE** (*Italian*). The major mode.

—— **MINORE** (*Italian*). The minor mode.

MODULATION. A change of key.

MODULAZIONE (*Italian*). Modulation.

MOLL (*German*). Minor in relation to modes and keys. *A moll,* A minor ; *H moll,* B minor.

MOLLEMENTE *Italian*). Softly, effeminately.

MOLTO *(Italian)*. Ver,, extremely: as,

———— ADAGIO *(Italian)*. Extremely slow

———— ALLEGRO *(Italian)*. Very quick.

———— MOSSO *(Italian)*. With much emotion.

———— SOSTENUTO *(Italian)*. In a very sustained manner.

MONFERINA *(Italian)*. The name of a very lively dance in ⅜ time.

MONOCHORD. An instrument with one string, for elucidating the doctrine of intervals.

MONOCORDE, à *(French)*. } On only one string.
MONOCORDO *(Italian)*.

MONODIA *(Italian)*. A term anciently applied to a melody
MONODIE *(Italian)*. } intended to be performed by a
MONODY. single voice.

MONTANT *(French)*. Ascending.

MORCEAU *(French)*. A piece or musical composition of any kind.

MORDENTE *(Italian)*. A beat or transient shake.

MORENDO *(Italian)*. Gradually subsiding in regard to tone and time; dying away.

MORISCO *(Italian)*. In the Moorish style.

MORMORANDO *(Italian)*. With a gentle, murmuring sound.

MOSSO *(Italian)*. Movement; as, *più mosso*, with more movement, quicker; *meno mosso*, slower.

MOSTRA *(Italian)*. A direct.

MOTET } A sacred composition of the anthem
MOTETTO *(Italian)*. } kind.

MOTIVO *(Italian)* The principal subject of an air, or other musical composition.

MOTO, con *(Italian)*. With agitation, anxiously

MOTO CONTRARIO (*Italian*). In contrary movement.
A term used in counterpoint to imply that the melody of
one part moves in an opposite direction to that of another.

MOTTEGGIANDO (*Italian*). Jeeringly, jocosely.

MOTUS (*Latin*). Motion ; as,

———— CONTRARIUS (*Latin*). Contrary motion.

———— OBLIQUUS (*Latin*). Oblique motion.

———— RECTUS (*Latin*). Similar or direct motion.

MOVIMENTO (*Italian*). Time, movement.

MUSETTE (*French*). A small kind of bagpipe ; also an
air of a sweet and pastoral character.

MUSIC. The language of sounds.

MUSICO (*Italian*). A musician ; also the name applied to
those male vocalists who formerly sang the soprano parts in
operas, &c.

MUTE. A small instrument which is occasionally placed on
the bridge of a violin, tenor, or violoncello, to damp or diminish the tone of the instrument, by checking its vibrations.

N.

NACCARE (*Italian*). The castagnets.

NACHAHMUNG (*German*). Imitation.

NACHDRUCK (*German*). Emphasis, accent.

NACHSPIEL (*German*). A postlude, or piece played after
some other.

NACHSTVERWANDTE TÖNE (*German*). Nearest relative keys.

NASAL TONE. In singing, this term implies that the voice
is deteriorated by passing through the nostrils

NASARD. An organ-stop, tuned a twelfth above the Diapasons.

NATURAL. A character marked ♮, used to contradict a sharp or flat.

NATURAL MODULATION. That which is confined to the key of the piece and its relatives.

NEAPOLITAN SIXTH. A chord composed of a minor third and minor sixth, which is situated on the fourth degree of the scale. In the key of C major or minor this chord is as follows:

       D ♭
       A ♭
       F

NEBENGEDANKEN (*German plural*). Accessory and subordinate ideas.

NEGLIGENTE (*Italian*).
NEGLIGENTEMENTE (*Italian*). } Negligently, without
NEGLIGENZA, con (*Italian*). } straint.

NEGLI (*Italian*).
NEI (*Italian*).
NEL (*Italian*).
NELLA (*Italian*). } In the.
NELLE (*Italian*).
NELLO (*Italian*).

NETTAMENTE (*Italian*). } Neatly.
NETTO (*Italian*).

NEUVIÈME (*French*). The interval of a ninth

NIEDERSCHLAG (*German*). The accented part of a bar

NOBILE (*Italian*). } With nobleness and grandeur
NOBILMENTE (*Italian*).

NOCTURNE (*French*). See NOTTURNO.

NOELS. The name given by the French to their Christmas carols.

NOIRE (*French*). A crotchet.

NON (*Italian*). An adverb of negation, generally associa'ed with *troppo*, as,

NON TROPPO ALLEGRO (*Italian*). } Not too quick.
NON TROPPO PRESTO (*Italian*). }

NONA (*Italian*). The interval of a ninth.

NONETTO (*Italian*). A composition in nine parts.

NON MOLTO (*Italian*). Not much.

NON TANTO (*Italian*). Not too much; moderately; as, *allegro non tanto*, moderately quick.

NOTA (*Italian*). A note; as,

—— BUONA (*Italian*). A strong or accented note.

—— CAMBIATA (*Italian*). A changed or irregularly transient note.

—— CARATTERISTICA *Italian*). A characteristic or leading note.

—— CATTIVA (*Italian*). A weak or unaccented note.

—— DI PASSAGIO (*Italian*). } A passing note, or note
NOTE DE PASSAGE (*French*). } of regular transition.

NOTA D'ABELLIMENTO (*Italian*). } A note of irregular
NOTE D'AGREMENT (*French*). } transition.

NOTA SENSIBILE (*Italian*). } The leading note of the
NOTA SENSIBILIS (*Latin*). } scale, or that note of the
NOTE SENSIBLE (*French*). } scale which is situated a semitone below the key note.

NOTATION. The art of representing musical sounds and their various modifications by notes, signs, terms, &c.

NOTAZIONE MUSICALE (*Italian*). Musical notation.

NOTENPLAN (*German*). The stave.

NOTES DE GOUT (*French*). Notes of embellishment.

NOTTURNO (*Italian*). A composition, vocal or instrumental, suitable for evening recreation, from its elegance and lightness of character.

NUOVO, *di* (*Italian*). Newly; again.

O.

O (*Italian*). Or; as, *flauto o violino*, flute or violin.

OBBLIGATI (*Italian plu*). ⎱ A part or parts of a composition
OBBLIGATO (*Italian*). ⎰ indispensable to its just performance, and which, therefore, cannot properly be omitted.

OBLIQUE. A term applied to that relative motion between
two parts, where the one ascends or descends,
other remains stationary.

OBOE (*Italian*). The hautboy, or hautboys.

OBOISTA (*Italian*). A performer on the oboe.

OCTAVE. An interval of eight notes.

OCTUOR (*French*). A piece in eight parts.

ODEUM (*Greek*). A place for the public performance of
music; a concert room or hall.

ŒUVRE (*French*). Opera or work; as, *œuvre premier*, the
first work, &c.

OFFERTOIRE (*French*). ⎱
OFFERTORIUM (*Latin*). ⎰ A part of the Catholic morning
OFFERTORY. ⎰ service.

OHNE (*German*) Without: as, *ohne begleitungen*, without
accompaniments.

ONDEGGIAMENTO (*Italian*). With a waving, tremulous
motion of the sound; as also, on the violin, tenor, &c. a
close shake.

OPEN DIAPASON. An organ stop, so called from its
pipes being open at the top. It is tuned to the same pitch
as the pianoforte, &c.

OPEN HARMONY. Harmony in which the notes are
separated by wide intervals.

OPERA (*Italian*). A musical drama, consisting of recita-tives, airs, choruses, &c. combined with scenery, decorations, and action. This term is also applied to any publication or work of an author.

OPERA BUFFA (*Italian*). A comic opera.

———— **SEMI-SERIA** (*Italian*). A semi-serious opera.

———— **SERIA** (*Italian*). A serious or tragic opera.

OPERETTA (*Italian*). A short or little opera.

OPHICLEIDE. A brass instrument lately introduced into this country, of a loud tone and a deep pitch. It is chiefly used in military music.

ORATORIO (*Italian*). A musical drama, founded on some Scriptural story, performed without the aid of scenery and action.

ORCHESTRA (*Italian*). That enclosed part of the theatre, between the stage and the audience, which is occupied by the musicians or instrumental performers. Sometimes, also, it is applied to designate, collectively, the performers tnem-selves; as, a full orchestra, a thin orchestra.

ORDINARIO (*Italian*). Usual; as, *a tempo ordinario,* is the usual time.

ORECCHIA (*Italian*). ⎫ The ear.
ORECCHIO (*Italian*). ⎭

ORECCHIA MUSICALE (*Italian*). ⎫ A musical ear.
OREILLE MUSICALE (*French*). ⎭

ORGAN. ⎫ A well-known and highly appreci-
ORGANO (*Italian*). ⎪ ated musical instrument, **chiefly**
ORGEL (*German*). ⎬ used in churches, and other **places**
ORGUE (*French*). ⎭ of divine worship. *

ORGANI VOCALI (*Italian*). The vocal organs.

---

* For a history and description of this most noble of all instruments see Hamilton's Organ Catechism, new edition by Joseph Warren.

ORGAN-POINT. A pedal note, or stationary bass.

ORGANUM (*Latin*). An ancient species of counterpoint fourths, fifths, and octaves

ORGELGEHÄUSE (*German*). The case of an organ.

ORGEL SCHÜLE (*German*). A school or method for th organ.

ORGEL STÜCKE (*German*). Pieces for the organ.

ORGELPUNKT (*German*). An organ-point or pedal note.

ORNAMENTI (*Italian*). } Graces; as the appoggiatura,
ORNEMENS (*French*). } turn, shake, &c.

OSSERVANZA, con (*Italian*). With scrupulous exactness in regard to time.

OSSIA (*Italian*). Or else; as *ossia più facile*, or else in this more easy manner.

OSTINATO (*Italian*). Persevered in, adhered to, continued in despite of circumstances.

OTTAVA, or 8*va* (*Italian*). An octave. This word is generally joined with *alta* or *bassa*: the first signifies that the passage to which it is applied must be played an octave higher than it is written; the second that it must be played an octave lower.

OTTAVINA (*Italian*). The little or higher octave.

OTTETTO (*Italian*). A composition in eight parts.

OUIE (*French*). The hearing.

OUVERTURE (*French*). } An overture, or introductory
OVERTURA (*Italian*). } symphony to a dramatic performance.

P.

PANDEAN PIPES. } One of the most ancient and simple of
PAN'S PIPES. } musical instruments; made of reeds of different lengths, stopped at the bottom, and blown by mouth at the top.

PANTALON *(French)*. One cf the movements of the quadrille. Also the name of an instrument of the dulcimer species, but larger, and played in the same manner.

PARALLEL MOTION. When two parts continue on the same degree and only repeat the same sounds, they are said to be in *parallel motion*.

PARFAIT *(French)*. Perfect, with regard to intervals, &c.

PARLANDO *(Italian)*. In a speaking or declamatory manner.

PARLANTE *(Italian)*. Accented, as if with words, in a declamatory style.

PARTE *(Italian)*. A part in vocal or instrumental music.

————— CANTANTE *(Italian)*. The singing or vocal part.

PARTIE *(French)*. A part in a composition.

PARTIMENTI *(Italian plural)*. Preparatory exercises for the study of harmony and accompaniment.*

PARTITION *(French)*. ⎫
PARTITUR *(German)*. ⎪ A score or entire draught of a
PARTITURA *(Italian)*. ⎬ composition in several parts.
PARTIZIONE *(Italian)*. ⎭

- AS *(French)*. A dance; as *pas seul, pas de deux*, a dance by one, or by two performers; *pas redoublé*, a quick step.

PASSACAGLIO *(Italian)*. ⎫ A slow dance in $\frac{3}{4}$ time.
PASSACAILLE *(French)*. ⎬

PASSAGGIO *(Italian)*. A passage or series of quick notes.

PASSEPIED. An old French dance in $\frac{3}{8}$ or $\frac{3}{4}$ time.

PASSING NOTES. Notes foreign to the harmony, but which serve to connect those which are essential.

See the Exercise in Fétis' "*Elementary and Abridged Method of Harmony and Accompaniment*," extr   the Partimenti of Fenaroli, Sala, &c.

PASSIONATAMEN rE (*Italian*). } In an impassioned man-
PASSIONATE (*Italian*). } ner.

PASSIONATO (*Italian*). } Impassioned, with pathos.
PASSIONE, con (*Italian*). }

ASSIONE (*Italian*). The passion, or seven last words of
our Saviour, set to music.

PATETICO (*Italian*). } Pathetically.
PATHETIQUE (*French*). }

PASTICCIO (*Italian*). } An opera made up of songs by dif-
PASTICHE (*French*). } ferent masters.

PASTORALE (*Italian*). } In a pastoral style. Also, a soft
PASTORELLA (*Italian*). } and rural movement.

PASTOURELLE (*French*) One of the movements of the
quadrille.

PAUKEN (*German plur.*). The kettle drums.

PAUSA (*Italian*). A rest.

PAUSA GENERALE (*Italian*). } A pause for all the per-
PAUSE GÉNÉRALE (*French*). } formers.

PAUSE (*French*). A semibreve, or whole bar's rest.

PAUSE (*German*). A rest.

PAUSE. A musical character, consisting of a dot surmounted
by a curve, which serves to protract the duration of a note or
rest beyond its natural value.

PAVANE (*French*). An antiquated French dance of a serious
cast.

PEDALE (*Italian*). A pedal or stationary bass. In piano
music, this term implies that the performer must press down
the pedal which takes off the dampers.

PEDALE (*German*). That set of keys belonging to an organ
which are played on by the feet.*

* See André and Hamilton's Treatise on the Management of the
Pedale.

I 2

PEDALI (*Italian*). The pedals in piano or organ music.

PEDALIERA (*Italian*). The pedal keys of an organ, spoken of collectively.

PENTACHORD. A scale of five diatonic degrees.

PENTATONON (*Greek*). An interval of five whole tones, or the augmented sixth.

PER (*Italian*). For or by; as *per il violino*, for the violin.

PERCUSSIONE (*Italian*). Percussion, or the act of striking a note or chord.

PERDENDO (*Italian*).
PERDENDOSI (*Italian*). } These terms imply a gradual diminution, both in the quantity
PERDEN (*abbrev.*)   of tone and speed of movement.

PERFECT. A term applied by theorists to certain intervals and chords.

PERFECT CADENCE. A complete and satisfactory close in both the harmony and melody.

PERFECT CONCORDS. } The perfect fourth, fifth,
PERFECT CONSONANCES. } and eighth.

PERFETTO (*Italian*). Perfect, with regard to intervals, &c.

PERIOD.
PERIODE (*French*). } A complete musical sentence containing several members.
PERIODO (*Italian*).

PERIODENBAU (*German*). The construction of musica periods.

PESANTE (*Italian*). With importance and weight, impressively.

PETITE MESURE À DEUX TEMS (*French*). $\frac{2}{4}$ time.

PEU (*French*). A little.

PEZZE (*Italian plur.*). Fragments, select detached pieces of music.

PHONICS. The art of treating musical sounds, either singly or in combination.

PHRASE. A short musical sentence containing an incomplete idea.*

PHRYGIAN. The name of one of the ancient modes.

PIACERE (*Italian*). Will, pleasure: as, *à piacere* at the performer's pleasure in regard to time.

PIACEVOLE (*Italian*).
PIACEVOLEZZA, con (*Italian*). } Agreeably; in a pleasing and graceful style.
PIACEVOLMENTE (*Italian*).

PIANGENDO (*Italian*). Plaintively.

PIANGEVOLE (*Italian*). } Despondingly, dolefully.
PIANGEVOLMENTE (*Italian*). } fully.

PIANISSIMO or *pp.* (*Italian*). Extremely soft.

PIANO, or *p.* (*Italian*). Soft.

———— A QUEUE (*French*). A grand pianoforte.

———— CARRÉ (*French*). A square pianoforte.

PIANOFORTE SCHOOL. A copious book of instruction for the piano.

PIANOFORTE SCORE. A score containing the vocal parts of a composition, with a pianoforte arrangement of the instrumental parts.

PIANOGRAPHE. A highly ingenious machine, invented by M. Guerin, which on being attached to the pianoforte indicates, on paper prepared for the purpose, anything played by the pianist.

PIATTI (*Italian plur.*) The cymbals.

PICCIOLO (*Italian*). } Little: as, *violino picciolo*, a small
PICCOLO (*Italian*). } violin: *flauto-piccolo*, a small flute.

PICHETTATO, (*Italian*). } In violin playing, these terms
PIQUÉ (*French*). } signify that species of *staccato* indicated by dots surmounted with a slur.

---

* See Hamilton's Musical Grammar, as also his Catechism on the Invention, Exposition, Development, and Concatenation of Musical Ideas.

PIEDS (*French*). The feet: as, *avec les pieds*, with the feet in organ playing.

PIENA (*Italian*). Full: as *à piena orchestra*, for a full orchestra.

PIENO (*Italian*). Full.

PIETOSAMENTE (*Italian*).{ With pity, compassionately.
PIETOSO (*Italian*).

PIFFERO (*Italian*). A fife.

PIÙ (*Italian*). An adverb of augmentation: as

—— FORTE. Louder.

—— LENTO. Slower.

—— PIANO. Softer.

—— PRESTO. Quicker.

PIÙ TOSTO (*Italian*). Rather; as,

—— ———— ALLEGRO. Rather quick.

PIVA (*Italian*). A bagpipe.

PIZZICATO or PIZZ. (*Italian*). In violin or violoncello music, is applied to notes which are to be twitched with the finger, instead of being played with the bow.

PLACIDAMENTE (*Italian*). With placidity, quietly.

PLAGAL. The name applied to those *church modes* whose melody was confined within the limits of the dominant and its octave.

PLAGAL-CADENCE. The triad on the key-note preceded by that on the subdominant.

PLAIN CHANT (*French*). Plain song or chant.

PLANTIVO (*Italian*). Expressively, plaintively.

PLAQUÉ (*French*). Struck at once, in speaking of chords.

PLECTRUM. A piece of quill or ivory, used to twitch the strings of the mandoline, &c. instead of the fingers.

PLEIN JEU (*French*). Full organ.

PLUS (*French*). More: as, *plus animé*, with greater animation.

PNEUMATIC. A term applied to wind instruments in gene
ral.

POCHETTE (*French*). A kit or small violin used by dancing
masters.

POCHETTINO (*Italian*). } A little: as *ritard. un pochettin*
POCHETTO (*Italian*)   } play somewhat slower.

POCO (*Italian*). A little, rather, somewhat: as

——— ANIMATO. Rather animated.

——— MENO. Somewhat less.

——— PIANO. Somewhat soft.

——— PIÙ. Somewhat more.

——— PRESTO. Rather quick.

POCO A POCO (*Italian*). By degrees, gradually; as,

——— — ——— CRESCENDO. Louder and louder by
degrees.

——— — ——— DIMINUENDO. Softer and softer by
degrees.

POGGIATO (*Italian*). Dwelt upon, impressive.

POI (*Italian*). Then; as *piano poi forte*, soft, then loud.

POINT (*French*). A dot.

POINT D'ORGUE (*French*). A pause; also a pedal pas
sage.

POINTEE (*French*). Dotted, in speaking of the duration of
notes.

POLACCA (*Italian*).   ⎰ A slow Polish dance in ¾ time. f
POLONAISE (*French*). ⎱ a peculiar rhythmical constru-
POLONOISE (*French*). ⎰ tion, as the melodial ment. s
usually terminate on the third crotchet of the bar.

POLKA. A tolerably quick Bohemian dance in ¾ time.

POLYMORPHOUS. Having many forms: generally used
in reference to *canons*.

POMPOSO (*Italian*). In a grand and pompous manner

PONTICELLO (*Italia*, The bridge, in speaking of the violin, guitar, &c.

PONCTUATION MUSICALE (*French*). Musical punctuation or phrasing.

PORTANDO LA VOCE (*Italian*). Sustaining the voice.

PORTAMENTO (*Italian*). The manner of sustaining and conducting the voice. A gliding from one note to another.

PORTAR LA VOCE (*Italian*). }
PORTER LA VOIX (*French*). } To sustain the voice.

PORT-DE-VOIX (*French*). An appoggiatura.

PORTÉE (*French*). The stave on which the notes are written.

POSATO (*Italian*). Quietly, steadily.

POSAUNE (*German*). The trombone.

POSITION (*French*). A position or shift, on the violin, tenor, or violoncello.

POSITIF (*French*). }
POSITIV (*German*). } The choir organ.

POSSIBILE (*Italian*). Possible; as *il più forte possibile*, as loud as possible.

POST-HORN (*German*). A sort of bugle; also a movement suited to, and imitating the notes of such an instrument.

POTPOURRI (*French*). A capriccio or fantasia on favorite airs.

POULE (*French*). One of the movements of the quadrille.

POUR (*French*). For.

POUSSÉ (*French*). In violin or violoncello music this term is used to indicate an up-bow.

PRALL-TRILLER (*German*). A transient shake marked thus ⚡

PRATICO (*Italian*). Practical.

PRECENTOR. The leader of the choir.

PREGHIERA (*Italian*) A prayer.

PRECIPITAMENTE (*Italian*).
PRECIPITATO (*Italian*).
PRECIPITAZIONE, *con* (*Italian*).
PRECIPITOSO (*Italian*).
} In a hurried manner

PRECIPITÉ (*French*). Hurried, accelerated.

PRECISIONE (*Italian*). With precision, exactitude.

PRELUDIO (*Italian*).
PRELUDIUM (*Latin*).
} A prelude or introductory move-ment.

PREMIÈRE (*French*). First; as *première fois*, first time.

PREPARATION. A term in harmony relating to disso nances. It consists in causing the dissonant note to be heard as a consonance in the preceding chord in the same part of the harmony.

PREPARAZIONE (*Italian*). The preparation of a disso nance.

PRESTAMENTE (*Italian*). Hurriedly, rapidly.

PRESTEZZA (*Italian*). Rapidity, quickness; as, *con pres tezza*, with rapidity.

PRESTISSIMO (*Italian*). The most rapid degree of move ment.

PRESTO (*Italian*). Very quick.

PRIMA BUFFA (*Italian*). First comic actress and singer
—— DONNA (*Italian*). The principal female singer in an Italian opera.
—— VISTA (*Italian*). At first sight.
—— VOLTA (*Italian*). First time.

PRIMO (*Italian*). First; as, *violino primo*, first violin; *tempo primo*, in the first or original time.
—— BUFFO (*Italian*). First comic actor and singer.
—— MUSICO (*Italian*). Principal male singer.

PRINCIPAL. An organ stop tuned an octave above the diapasons.*

---

* See Hamilton's Organ Catechism for a description of all the numerous stops.

PRINCIPALE (*Italian*). Principal; as, *violino principale*, the principal violin.

PRINCIPALMENTE (*Italian*). Principally

PROBE (*German*). ⎱
PROVA (*Italian*). ⎰ A rehearsal.

PRONUNZIARE (*Italian*). To pronounce.

PROPOSTA (*Italian*). The subject of a fugue.

PSALM. ⎱
PSEAUME (*French*). ⎰ A sacred song.

PUNKT (*German*). A dot.

PULSATILE. A term applied to such instruments as are made to sound by being struck upon, as a drum, a tambourine, &c.

PUNKTIRTE NOTEN (*German*). Dotted notes.

PUNTA (*Italian*). The point; as, *colla punta dell' arco*, with the point or tip of the bow.

PUNTATO (*Italian*). Pointed, detached.

PUPITRE (*French*). A music-desk.

Q.

QUADRICINIUM. A composition in four parts.

QUADRILLE (*French*). A French dance, or rather, a set of five consecutive dance movements, called *Le Pantalon, La Poule, L'Ete, La Trenise ou La Pastourelle, La Finale.*

QUADRUPLE COUNTERPOINT. Counterpoint in four parts, all of which are invertible.

QUADRUPLE CROCHE (*French*). A semidemisemiquaver.

QUARTA (*Italian*). ⎱
QUARTE (*French* and *German*) ⎰ The interval of a fourth

QUARTA TONI (*Italian*). ⎱ The subdominant, or fourth
QUARTE DU TON (*French*). ⎰ note of the scale.

QUARTER-NOTE. A crotchet (♩

QUART DE TON (*French*). } That sligh. difference of
QUARTER-TONE. } pitch made on the vio-
QUARTO DI TUONO (*Italian*). } lin, &c., between E
sharp and D flat, or the like.

QUART-DE-SOUPIR (*French*). } A semiquaver rest.
QUARTO D'ASPETTO (*Italian*). }

QUARTETT. } A composition for four voices or
QUARTETTO (*Italian*). } instruments.

QUASI (*Italian*). In the manner or style of: as, *quasi alle-gretto*, like an *allegretto*.

QUATUOR (*French*). A quartet or composition for four voices or instruments.

QUAVER. A note equal in duration to the half of a crotchet.

QUEERSTRICHE (*German*). Ledger lines

QUESTO (*Italian*). This; that.

QUEUE (*French*). The tail-piece of a violin, tenor, &c.

QUIETO (*Italian*). With calmness or repose; quietly.

QUINTA (*Italian*). } The interval of a fifth.
QUINTE (*French* and *German*). }

QUINTETT. } A composition for five voices or
QUINTETTO (*Italian*). } instruments.
QUINTUOR (*French*). }

QUI TOLLIS (*Latin*). A movement of the Gloria.

QUODLIBET. A term sometimes applied to a certain species of composition written in a comic style.

QUONIAM TU SOLUS (*Latin*). Part of the Gloria.

R.

R. or **R. H.** indicates the right hand in pianoforte music.
RABBIA, con (*Italian*). With rage, furiously.
RADDOLCENDO (*Italian*). } With augmented softness
RADDOLCENTE (*Italian*). }

RADDOPPIAMENTO (*Italian*). ⎫ The doubling of an in-
REDOUBLEMENT (*French*). ⎭ terval.

RADICAL BASS. The fundamental bass.

RALLENTANDO (*Italian*). Implies a gradual diminution
in the speed of the movement, and a corresponding decrease
in the quantity of tone.

RANZ DES VACHES (*French*). Airs played upon their
pipes by the Swiss herdsmen, to assemble their herds and
keep them together on their return home.

RAPIDAMENTE (*Italian*). ⎫
RAPIDITÀ, *con* (*Italian*). ⎬ Rapidly, with rapidity.
RAPIDO (*Italian*). ⎭

RATTENENDO (*Italian*). Restraining or holding back the
time.

RAVVIVANDO (*Italian*). Reviving, reanimating, accelerating; as *ravvivando il tempo*, animating or quickening the
time.

RE. A syllable applied in solfaing to the note D.

REBEC. A Moorish instrument with two strings, to which
the Spaniards added a third.

RECHEAT. The name by which huntsmen designate those
sounds which are played on the horn to recal the hounds
from a false scent.

RECHT (*German*). Right; as, *rechte Hand*, the right hand

RECITANDO (*Italian*). In the style of recitation; decla
matory.

RECITANTE (*Italian*). In the style of a recitative.

RECITATIF (*French*). A recitative.

RECITATIVO (*Italian*). A recitative or musical declamati
—————— SECCO (*Italian*). Unaccompanied reci
tive.
—————— STROMENTATO (*Italian*). Recita
accompanied by the orchestra.

R E ED The mouth-piece of the hautboy, English horn, and bassoon, formed of two pieces of cane joined in a peculiar manner. Also the flat piece of cane placed on the beak of the clarinet, and the small pieces of metal through which the wind passes into some organ pipes.

REEL. A lively Scotch dance.

REFRAIN (*French*). A burden, or tag-end to a song.

REGINA CŒLI (*Latin*). A hymn to the Virgin.

REGISTER (*German*). An organ stop.

REGLE (*French*). ⎫ A rule or precept for composition or
REGOLA (*Italian*). ⎬ performance.

REGLE DE L'OCTAVE (*French*). A formula which shews the method of harmonizing or accompanying the ascending or descending scale taken as a bass.

REGULAR MOTION. Similar motion.

REHEARSAL. A trial or practice, previous to a public performance.

RELATIVE KEYS. Keys which differ only by having in their scales one sharp or flat more or fewer.

RELIGIOSAMENTE (*Italian*). ⎫ With religious feeling ;
RELIGIOSO (*Italian*). ⎬ a devotional manner.

RENVERSEMENT (*French*). An inversion.

RENVOI (*French*). A mark of repetition.

RÉPÉTITION (*French*). A rehearsal.

REPETIZIONE (*Italian*). Repetition ; as, *senza repetizione*, without repetition.

REPLICA (*Italian*). Repetition; as *senza replica*, without repetition ; *con replica*, with repetition.

REPLICATO (*Italian*). Repeated.

RÉPONSE (*French*). The answer of a fugue.

REPRISE (*French*). A repetition or return to some preceding part.

REPRISE D'UN OPERA (*French*). The representation of an opera which has not been given for some time.

REQUIEM (*Latin*). A musical service for the dead.

RESOLUTION. The concord which necessarily follows a preceding discord is called its resolution.

RESPIRO (*Italian*). A semiquaver rest.

RESTS. The characters which indicate silence in music.

RETARDATION. The continuation of one or more notes of a chord into the following chord.

RETROGRADO (*Italian*). In retrograde movement.

RETTO (*Italian*). Direct; as, *moto retto*, direct or similar motion.

RHAPSODIE (*French*). A rhapsody, a capriccio.

RHYTHM. The theory of musical cadence, as applied to melody.

RICERCARI (*Italian plural*). Difficult exercises for the voice or for some instrument.

RICERCATA (*Italian*). A fugue replete with contrapuntal artifices.

RICORDANZA (*Italian*). With recollection, remembrance.

RIDOTTO (*Italian*). Adapted, arranged; also, an entertainment consisting of singing and dancing.

RIFFIORIMENTI (*Italian plural*). Extemporaneous embellishments.

RIGADOON. An antiquated French dance in triple time.

RINFORZANDO (*Italian*).
RINFORZATO (*Italian*). } With additional tone and emphasis.
RINFORZO (*Italian*).
RINF. or RF. (*abbrev*).

RIPIENO (*Italian*). A term applied to such parts in concerted music, as are intended to fill up and augment the effect of the *tutti*, or full chorus of voices or instruments.

RIPRESA (*Italian*). A mark of repetition.

RISOLUTAMENTE (*Italian*).
RISOLUTO (*Italian*).
RISOLUZIONE, con (*Italian*). } With boldness and resolu-lution.

RISOLUTISSIMO (*Italian*). With extreme resolution.

RISOLUZIONE (*Italian*). The resolution of a discord.

RISPOSTA (*Italian*). The answer of a fugue.

RISVEGLIATO (*Italian*). With much animation.

RISVEGLIARE (*Italian*). To re-animate the execution.

RITARDANDO (*Italian*).
RITARDATO (*Italian*). } Implies a gradual retarding or slackening of the time, with a corresponding diminution in point of tone.

RITARDO (*Italian*). A retardation.

RITENENDO (*Italian*).
RITENENTE (*Italian*).
RITENUTO (*Italian*). } A keeping back, a decrease in the speed of the movement.

RITORNELLO (*Italian*). A short symphony or introduction to an air; as also the symphonies between the members or periods of the air. The same term is applied, also, to the *tutti* parts, introductory to, and between the solos of a concerto.

RIVOLGIMENTO (*Italian*). The inversion of the parts in double counterpoint.

RIVOLTATO (*Italian*). Inverted.

RIVOLTO (*Italian*). An inversion.

ROHR (*German*). A reed.

ROHRWERK (*German*). Reed-work: the reed-stops of an organ taken collectively.

ROLLO (*Italian*).
ROLLANDO (*Italian*).
ROULEMENT (*French*). } The roll on the drum and tambourine.

ROMANCE (*French*).
ROMANZA (*Italian*). } A short lyric tale, set to music, or simple and elegant melody suitable to such words.

ROMANESQUE (*French*). A dance tune; called also *Gal liard*.

RÖMISCHE GESANG (*German*). The plain chant of the Catholic service.

RONDE (*French*). A semibreve.

RONDEAU (*French*). ⎫ A rondo or composition of several
RONDO (*Italian*). ⎬ strains or members, at the end of each of which the first part or subject is repeated.

RONDILETTA (*Italian*). ⎫
RONDINETTO (*Italian*). ⎬ A short rondo.
RONDINO (*Italian*). ⎬
RONDOLETTO (*Italian*). ⎭

ROOT. The fundamental note of any chord.

ROSALIA (*Italian*). The repetition of a passage several times over, each time ascending one degree.

ROTE. The old name of the hurdy-gurdy.

ROTONDO (*Italian*). Round or full, as regards tone.

ROULADE (*French*). A division or rapid flight of notes.

ROUND. A sort of canon in the unison.

ROUNDELAY. A sort of antique poem, in various parts of which a return is made to the first verse or couplet A poetical rondo.

ROVESCIO, (*Italian*). Inverted, reverted

RUBATO (*Italian*). Robbed, borrowed. The terms *tempo rubato* are applied to a style of performance in which some notes are held longer than their legitimate time, while others are curtailed of their proportionate duration, in order that, on the whole, the aggregate value of the bar may not be disturbed.

RÜCKUNG (*German*). Syncopation.

RUHEPUNCT (*German*). A point of repose in melody; a cadenc .

RUSSE (*French*). Russian; as, *à la Russe*, in the Russian style.

S.

SACKBUT. An old-fashioned instrument, resembling a trombone.

SAGGIO (*Italian*). An essay.

SAITE (*German*). A string of a musical instrument.

SAITENHALTER (*German*). The tail-piece of a violin, tenor, &c.

SALMO (*Italian*). A psalm.

SALTANDO (*Italian*). Proceeding by skips or bounds.

SALTERELLA. See Sartarella.

SALTERIO (*Italian*). } A psalter, or book of psalms.
SALTERO (*Italian*). }

SALTO (*Italian*). A leap or skip.

SALVE REGINA (*Latin*). A hymn to the Virgin.

SANCTUS (*Latin*). A principal movement of the mass or Catholic service.

SANFT (*German*). Soft; as, *mit sanften Stimmen*, with soft stops, in organ music.

SÄNGER (*German*). A singer.

SANS (*French*). Without; as, *sans pedales*, without the pedals, in organ playing.

SARABANDA (*Italian*) } A saraband, an antique low
SARABANDE (*French*). } dance-tune.

SARTARELLA (*Italian*). } A Neapolitan dance.
SARTARELLO (*Italian*). }

SATTEL (*German*). The nut of a violin finger-board, &c.

SBARRA DOPPIA (*Italian*). A double bar.

lian). A scale or gamut

SCALD. Among the Northern nations, implies a bard or poet-musician.

SCENA (*Italian*). A scene or portion of an opera. An act is generally composed of several scenes.

SCHERZANDO (*Italian*).
SCHERZANTE (*Italian*).
SCHERZEVOLMENTE (*Italian*).
SCHERZO (*Italian*).
SCHERZOSAMENTE (*Italian*).
SCHERZOSO (*Italian*).
SCHERZ. (*abbrev.*)
} In a light, playful, and sportive manner.

SCHERZANDISSIMO (*Italian*). In an exceedingly playful style.

SCHOTTISCHE (*German*). The name given to a rather slow modern dance in $\frac{2}{4}$ time:

SCHLEIFEZEICHEN (*German*). A slur.

SCHUSTERFLECK (*German*). Synonymous with *Rosalia* See that word.

SCHLÜSSEL (*German*). The clef.

SCHNARRPFEIFEN (*German*). Reed work, reed stops.

SCHNELL WALZER (*German*) Quick waltzes.

SCHREIBART (*German*). Style.

SCHULE (*German*). A school or method for learning an instrument, &c.

SCHWACH (*German*). Piano, or soft.

SCHWEIGE (*German*). A rest.

SCIOLTAMENTE (*Italian*). With freedom and agility.

SCIOLTO (*Italian*). With freedom and boldness.

SCOLARO (*Italian*). A scholar.

SCORE. An assemblage of the different parts of a composition, written on separate staves placed below each other. See FULL SCORE and PIANOFORTE SCORE.

SCOZZESE (*Italian*). In the Scotch style.

SDEGNO, *con* (*Italian*).
SDEGNOSAMENTE (*Italian*). } In a fiery and ndignæ style.
SDEGNOSO (*Italian*).

SDRUCCIOLARE (*Italian*). To slide; as by turning the finger-nails towards the keys of the pianoforte, and drawing the hand rapidly up or down.

SDRUCCIOLATO (*Italian*). Sliding the fingers along the keys or strings of an instrument.

SEC (*French*).
SECCO (*Italian*). } In a dry or unornamented manner.

SECHZEHNTHEIL NOTE (*German*). A semiquave

SECONDE (*French*). Second: as *seconde fois*, second time.

SECONDA (*Italian*). } The second.
SECONDO (*Italian*).

SECUNDE (*German*). The interval of a second.

SEGNO, or 𝄋: (*Italian*). A sign; as *al segno*, return to the sign; *dal segno*, repeat from the sign.

SEGUENDO (*Italian*). } Following.
SEGUENTE (*Italian*).

SEGUE (*Italian*). } Now follows, or as follows. Examples:
SEGUITO (*Italian*). } *segue il coro*, the chorus follows; *segue la finale*, the finale now follows. It is also used in the sense of *in similar* or *like manner*, to shew that a subsequent passage is to be played like that which precedes it.

SEGUIDILLA (*Spanish*). A favourite Spanish dance of three beats in a bar.

SEITENBEWEGUNG (*German*). Oblique motion.

SEIZIÈME DE SOUPIR (*French*). A semider quaver rest.

MI (*Latin*). Half: as, *semitone*, half a ton

SEMIBREVE. A long note equal to two minims. or four crotchets, &c.

SEMICHORUS. A chorus to be sung by only a portion of the voices.

SEMICHROMA (*Italian*). A semiquaver.

SEMIDEMISEMIQUAVER. A quadruple quaver, or a note having four tails, equal in duration to one half of a demi-semiquaver.

SEMIDIAPENTE (*Latin*). The diminished or imperfect fifth.

SEMIDITONE (*Latin*). The minor third.

SEMIFUSA (*Latin*). The ancient name fo a semiquaver.

SEMIMINIMA (*Latin*). A crotchet.

SEMITONE. A half tone.

SEMITONIUM MODI (*Latin*). The leading note.

SEMITUONO (*Italian*). A semitone.

SEMPLICE (*Italian*).
SEMPLICEMENTE (*Italian*). } With simplicity, artlessly.
SEMPLICITA, con (*Italian*).

SEMPRE (*Italian*). Always; *sempre staccato*, always staccato or detached; *sempre forte*, always loud; *sempre più forte*, continually increasing in force.

SENSIBILE (*Italian*). } With sensibility and feeling
SENSIBILITA, con (*Italian*).

SENSIBLE (*French*). The leading note or major seventh of the scale.

SENTIMENTALE (*Italian*). } With feeling and sentiment.
SENTIMENTO, con (*Italian*).

SENZA (*Italian*). Without; as *senza organo*, without the organ; *senza rigore*, without regard to exact time; *senza replica*, without repetition.

SEPTETTO (*Italian*). A septett, or piece for seven instruments.

SEPTETT. } A composition for seven voices or instru-
SEPTUOR. } ments.

SEPTIÈME (*French*). } The interva. of a seventh.
SEPTIME (*German*). }

SEQUENCE. A series of similar chords or intervals, &c

SEQUENZA (*Italian*). A sequence, or succession of similar chords on a uniform bass.

SERENADE (*French*). } A serenade or evening concert in
SERENATA (*Italian*). } the open air. This term is also used to designate any musical composition on an amorous subject, consisting of song, recitative, and chorus; or any light and pleasing instrumental composition consisting of several movements.

SERIA (*Italian*). Serious, tragic; as, *opera seria*, a serious opera.

SERIOSO (*Italian*). In a serious style.

SERPEGGIANDO (*Italian*). Gently and silently creeping onwards, quietly advancing.

SERPENT. } A military instrument, of a
SERPENTONO (*Italian*). } coarse, deep tone, somewhat resembling a serpent in its figure.

SERVICE. Certain portions of the Protestant Ritual when set to music are so called.

SESQUIALTERA. The name of an organ-stop composed of several ranks of pipes.

SESTA (*Italian*). The interval of a sixth.

SE ſETTO (*Italian*). } A vocal or instrumental composition
SESTETT. } in six parts.

SETTIMA (*Italian*). The interval of a seventh.

SETZART (*German*). Style of composition.

SETZKUNST (*German*). The art of musical composition.

SEVERAMENTE (*Italian*). } In a strict and severe style.
SEVERITÀ, con (*Italian*). }

SEXTE (*German*). The interval of a sixth.

SEXTUOR. A composition for six voices or instruments.

SFORZANDO (*Italian*). ⎫ Implies that a particular note is to
SFORZATO (*Italian*). ⎭ be played with emphasis and force.

SFUGGITO (*Italian*). *Avoided;* as, *Cadenza sfuggita,* an avoided (*i. e.,* a broken) cadence.

SHAWM. A wind instrument of the ancient Hebrews.

SI. A syllable applied in solfaing to the note B.

SICILIANA (*Italian*). A movement of a slow, soothing, pastoral character, in $\frac{6}{8}$ time, resembling the dance peculiar to the peasantry of Sicily.

SIEGUE. Properly Segue, which see.

SIGNATURE (*French*). The signature.

SIGNE (*French*). The :𝕊:, or direct.

SILENCE (*French*). A rest.

SIMILAR MOTION. That in which two or more parts always ascend or descend at the same time.

SIMILE (*Italian*). Similarly, in like manner.

SIMPLE INTERVALS. Such as do not exceed an octave.

SIMPLE TIMES. Those measures which contain but one principal accent; as, $\frac{2}{4}$, $\frac{3}{2}$, $\frac{3}{8}$, &c.

SINFONIA (*Italian*). ⎫ A symphony or orchestral composi
SINFONIE (*German*). ⎭ tion in many parts.

SINGHIOZZANDO (*Italian*). Sobbingly.

SINGLE CHANT. A simple harmonized melody extending only to one verse of a psalm as sung in cathedrals, &c.

SINGSCHULE (*German*). A singing school.

SINGSTIMMEN (*German plural*). The voices; the vocal parts.

SINISTRA (*Italian*). The left hand.

SINO (*Italian*). } As far as: as, con fuoco sin' al fine, with
SIN (*Italian*). } spirit to the end.

SI REPLICA (*Italian*). Repeat.

SISTRUM. An ancient Egyptian instrument of percussion.

SI TACE (*Italian*). Be silent.

SIX POUR QUATRE (*French*). A double triplet, or six notes to be played in the time of four.

SIXTE (*French*). The interval of a sixth.

SIXTEENTH NOTE. A semiquaver (♪)

SLENTANDO (*Italian*). A gradual diminution in the time :e speed of the movement.

LUR. A curved line drawn over two or more notes to indicate that they must be smoothly connected.

SMANICARE (*Italian*). To shift or change the position of the hand, in playing the violin and similar instruments.

SMANIOSO (*Italian*). With fury.

SMINUENDO (*Italian*). Gradually diminishing the sound.

SMORFIOSO (*Italian*). In an affected manner.

SMORZANDO (*Italian*). } A gradual diminution as to
SMORZATO (*Italian*). } tone.

SOAVE (*Italian*). } In a soft, sweet, delicate style.
SOAVEMENTE (*Italian*). }

SOGGETTO (*Italian*). The subject or theme.

SOL. A syllable applied in solfaing to the note G.

SOLA (*Italian*). Alone.

SOLENNEMENTE (*Italian*). } With solemnity.
SOLENNITA, con (*Italian*). }

SOLFA. } The practice of solfeggi by means of the syl-
SOLFAING. } lables do, re, mi, fa, sol, la, si, corresponding to the notes C, D, E, F, G, A, B.

SOLFEGE (*French*).
SOLFEGGI (*Italian plural*). } An exercise or exercises for the
SOLFEGGIO (*Italian*). } voice.

SOLI *(Italian plural)*. Implies that two or more principal parts play or sing together; such parts, of course, are never doubled.

SOLLECITO *(Italian)*. In an ardent, solicitous, and pensive style.

SOLMIZATION. The same as solfaing.

SOLO *(Italian)*. Alone.

SOLO *(Italian)*. A composition, or even a passage for a single voice or instrument, with or without accompaniments.

SONATA *(Italian)*. } A composition consisting of several
SONATE *(French)*. } movements, generally for a single principal instrument, with or without accompaniments.

SONATINA *(Italian)*. } A short and easy sonata.
SONATINE *(French)*. }

SONNET. A short poem of only fourteen lines.

SONORAMENTE *(Italian)*. } Sonorously; with a full vi
SONORITÀ, con *(Italian)*. } brating kind of tone.
SONORITÉ *(French)*. }

SONORE *(French)*. } Sonorous, full-toned.
SONORO *(Italian)*. }

SONS HARMONIQUES *(French plural)*. Harmonic sounds or notes.

SONS PLEINS *(French plural)*. Terms which often occur in flute music, and which indicate that the notes must be blown with a very full round tone.

SOPRA *(Italian)*. Above: as, *come sopra*, as above; *contrapunto sopra il soggetto*, counterpoint above the subject.

SOPRANO *(Italian)*. The highest species of female voice.

SORDAMENTE *(Italian)*. Damped, muffled.

SORDINI *(Italian plur.)* Mutes; as *con sordini*, with mutes, *senza sordini*, without mutes, on the violin, tenor, &c.

SORDINO *(Italian)*. A mute or damper applied to the bridge of the violin, nor, &c.

SOSPIRANDO (*Italian*). With apprehension, despondingly.

SOSPENSIONE (*Italian*). A suspension.

SOSPIRO (*Italian*). A crotchet rest.

SOSTENENDO. (*Italian*). } Sustained, continuous in regard
SOSTENUTO (*Italian*). to tone.
SOST. (*abbrev.*)

SOTTO (*Italian*). Below; as *contrapunto sotto il soggetto*, counterpoint below the subject.

OTTO VOCE (*Italian*). In an under-tone.

SOUPIR (*French*). A crotchet rest.

SOUSDOMINANTE (*French*). The subdominant or fourth of the scale.

SOUSMEDIANTE (*French*). The submediant or sixth of the scale.

SOUSTONIQUE (*Erench*). The seventh of the scale or sub-tonic.

SOUVENIRS (*French plural*). Recollections, reminiscences.

SPAZIO (*Italian*). A space of the stave.

SPIANATO (*Italian*). Smooth, even.

SPICCATO (*Italian*). Pointedly, distinctly. In violin music, this term implies that the notes are to be played with the point of the bow.

SPIELEN (*German*). To play upon an instrument.

SPINET. } An old keyed instrument.
SPINETTA (*Italian*).

SPIRITO, con (*Italian*).
SPIRITOSAMENTE. (*Italian*). } With spirit.
SPIRITOSO (*Italian*).

SPIRITUALE (*Italian*). Sacred.

SPONDEE. A musical foot consisting of two long notes

STA (*Italian*). } As it stands.
STAT (*Latin*)

STABAT MATER (*Latin*). A hymn on the Crucifixion.

STACCATISSIMO (*Italian*). Very detached.

STACCATO (*Italian*). This term implies that the notes to be played distinct, short, and detached from one another by rests.

STANGHETTA (*Italian*). A bar line.

STARK (*German*) *Forte*, loud; as, *mit starken Stimmen*, w loud stops, in organ playing.

STAVE. The five parallel lines on which the notes are placed.

STEG (*German*). The bridge of a violin, violoncello, &c.

STEM. The thin stroke which is drawn from the head of a note.

STENTATO (*Italian*). In a loud, bawling manner, for some particular effect.

STESSO (*Italian*). The same.

STHÉNOCHIRE. A machine for strengthening and imparting flexibility to the fingers, being a compound of the Dactylion and the Handguide.

STIBACCHIATO (*Italian*). Dragging, relaxing in the time.

STICCATO (*Italian*). A musical instrument, the sounds of which are produced by striking on little bars of wood.

STILO (*Italian*). Style, either of composition, or of performance.

STIMME (*German*). This word has various significations; as (*a*) the voice; (*b*) the sound-post of a violin, &c.; (*c*) a part in vocal or instrumental music; and (*d*) a stop of an organ.

STIMMSTOCK (*German*). The sound-post of a violin, &c.

STINGUENDO (*Italian*). Gradually diminishing the tone.

TRAIN. A portion of a movement divided off by a double bar.

STOPT DIAPASON. The name of an organ-stop; so called from having its pipes stopped at the top with a wooden plug, by which it is tuned. It is of the same pitch as the Open Diapason.

STRASCINANDO (*Italian*). }
STRASCINATO (*Italian*). } Dragging, relaxing in the
STRASCINIO, *con* (*Italian*). } degree of movement.

STRATHSPEY. A lively Scotch dance in common time.

STRENG (*German*). Strict, in relation to style.

STREPITOSAMENTE (*Italian*). }
STREPITO, *con* (*Italian*). } In a noisy, boisterous
STREPITOSO (*Italian*). } manner.

STRETTO (*Italian*). The knot. That part of a fugue in which the subject and answer succeed one another at a very short interval of time.* In modern music, it sometimes is used to imply an acceleration of the time near the close of the piece.

STRICHARTEN (*German plural*). Different ways of bowing.

STRINGENDO (*Italian*). Accelerating the degree of movement.

STRISCIANDO (*Italian*). Dragging in the time.

STROMENTI (*Italian plural*). Musical instruments in general as, *stromenti di vento*, wind instruments, &c.†

STUDIO (*Italian*). A vocal or instrumental exercise intended for the practice of some particular difficulty.

STUFE (*German*). A degree · as, *Stufe der Tonleiter*, a degree of the scale.

---

* See Cocks's magnificent edition of Albrechtsberger on Harmony and Composition, 2 vols.

† See Niemitz's Method for Musical Instruments, edited by A. Merrick.

SUAVE (*Italian*).
SUAVEMENTE (*Italian*). } With sweetness and delicacy a
SUAVITA, con (*Italian*). } expression.

SUB (*Latin*).　Under below.

SUBBASS (*German*)　A stop or set of pipes belonging to the pedals.

SUBDOMINANT.　The fourth note of the scale of any key.

UBITAMENTE (*Italian*) } Quickly: as *volti subito*, turn
SUBITO (*Italian*). } over quickly.

SUBMEDIANT.　The sixth of the scale.

SUBSEMITONE.　The semitone below the key-note.

SUBSEMITONIUM MODI (*Latin*).　The leading note.

SUBTONIC.　The note situated a semitone below the key-note.

SUDDEN MODULATION.　That in which the modulating chord is preceded by one which is not doubtful.　See GRA-DUAL MODULATION.

SUITE (*French*).　A series, a collection: as *une suite de pièces*, a series of lessons.

SUL (*Italian*).　On or upon: as *sul A*, on the A string of the violin, &c.; *sul ponticello*, on or near the bridge.

SUO LOCO (*Latin*).　In its own or usual place.

SUONO (*Italian*).　A sound.

SUPER (*Latin*).　Above, over.

SUPERDOMINANT.　The note next above the dominant in the scale.

SUPERFLUOUS INTERVALS.　Augmented intervals.

SUPERTONIC.　The note above the tonic or key-note.

SUPERTONIQUE (*French*).　The supertonic or second note of the scale.

SUR (*French*)　On: as *sur la quatrième corde*, on the fourth string.

SUSPENSION. The momentary withholding of a note by retaining some note of the previous chord.

SVEGLIATO (*Italian*). Smartly, with life.

SWELL. That portion of an organ which consists of a number of pipes enclosed in a box; with this box a pedal communicates, by which it may be gradually opened or shut, and thus the tone made louder and softer by degrees.*

SYMPHONIE (*French*). ⎫ A piece for a full orchestra. Also
SYMPHONY.　　　　 ⎭　 the instrumental parts which begin and end a song or other vocal composition.

SYNCOPATE (*Italian*). In a constrained and syncopated style.

SYNCOPATO (*Italian*). Syncopated.

SYNCOPATION. The connecting the last note of one bar to the first note of the next, so as to form but one note, of a duration equal to both: this displaces the accent and produces a peculiar effect.

SYNCOPE (*French*). A syncopation.

SYRINGA (*Latin*). Pans' pipes.

T.

TABLATURA (*Italian*). ⎫ That manner of writing a piece of
TABLATURE (*Italian*). ⎭　music formerly used for the theorbo, lute, &c., in which the sounds were expressed by letters instead of notes.

TABOR. A little drum used to accompany the pipe in rustic dances.

TABRET. One of the ancient Hebrew instruments mentioned in Scripture.

---

* See Hamilton's Catechism on the Organ

TACET (*Latin*). A word which implies that during a move ment, or part of a movement, some particular instrument is to be silent: as *flauto tacet*, the flute is not to play.

TAILLE (*French*). The tenor voice or part.

TAIL-PIECE. That piece of wood to which the strings of bow-instruments are fastened.

TAKT (*German*). The bar.

TAKTART (*German*). The species of time or measure.

TAKTSTRICH (*German*). The lines which mark the division of a piece into bars; the bar-line.

TALON (*French*). The heel of the bow, that part near the nut.

TAMBOUR (*French*). A military or great drum.

TAMBOURINE. A well-known pulsatile instrument, like the head of a drum, with jingles placed round it to increase the noise

TAMBURO (*Italian*). A drum.

TAMBURONE (*Italian*). The great drum.

TAMTAM. An Indian instrument of percussion like our tambourine.

TANTO (*Italian*). Not so much; not too much.

TANTUM ERGO (*Latin*). A hymn sung at the Benediction in the Catholic service.

TARDANDO (*Italian*). See RITARDANDO.

TARDO (*Italian*). Slowly, in a dragging manner.

TARANTELLA (*Italian*). A peculiar sort of dance, supposed to have the virtue of curing the bite of a venomous species of spider, called the tarantella.

TASTATUR (*German*). ⎫
TASTIERA (*Italian*). ⎬ The key-board of a pianoforte, &c.

TASTO SOLO. These words are used in organ and pianoforte music, to indicate that certain bass notes are not to be accompanied by chords in the right hand.

TEDESCA, *alla* (*Italian*). }
TEDESCO, *al* (*Italian*). } In the German style.

TE DEUM (*Latin*). A hymn of thanksgiving.

TEMA (*Italian*). A subject or theme.

TEMPERAMENT (*French*). Temperament, a term used in the mathematical theory of sound, in tuning, &c.*

TEMPESTOSO (*Italian*). In a tempestuous manner, violently agitated.

TEMPO (*Italian*). The degree of movement.

———— *a* or *in* (*Italian*). In time. An expression used after some relaxation in the measure, to indicate a return to the original degree of movement.

———— COMMODO (*Italian*). In a convenient degree of movement.

———— DI BALLO (*Italian*) In the time of a dance.

———— DI GAVOTTA (*Italian*). In gavot time.

———— DI MARCIA (*Italian*). In march time.

———— DI MENUETTO (*Italian*). In the time of a minuet.

———— DI VALSE (*Italian*). In the time of a waltz.

———— GIUSTO (*Italian*). In strict time.

———— PRIMO (*Italian*). In the first or original time.

———— RUBATO (*Italian*). Implies a slight deviation in the measure for the sake of expression, by protracting one note and curtailing another, so that the time of each bar is not altered in the aggregate.

TEMPS (*French*). } Time; also the various parts or divisions
TEMS (*French*). } of the bar; as,

TEMPS FOIBLE (*French*). The weak parts of the bar.

.EMPS FORT (*French*). The strong parts of the bar.

——— FRAPPÉ (*French*). The accented parts, or down beats.

——— LÉVÉ (*French*). The unaccented parts, or up-beats.

TENDREMENT (*French*). Affectionately, tenderly.

TENEBRÆ (*Latin plural*). The Catholic evening service during holy week.

TENERAMENTE (*Italian*). ⎱
TENEREZZA, con (*Italian*). ⎰ Tenderly.
TENERO (*Italian*).

TENIR (*French*). To hold, as a violin, a bow, &c.

TENORE (*Italian*). The tenor voice or tenor singer; a high male voice.

TENORSCHLÜSSEL (*German*). ⎱ The tenor clef.
TENORZEICHEN (*German*). ⎰

TENSILE. Such instruments as have strings are so called.

TENUTE (*Italian*). ⎱ Implies that a note or notes must be
TENUTO (*Italian*). ⎰ held on, sustained, or kept down
TEN. (*abbrev.*)   the full time.

TEORETICO (*Italian*). A theorist.

TEORIA (*Italian*). Theory.

TEPIDAMENTE (*Italian*). ⎱ With coldness and
TEPIDITÀ, con (*Italian*). ⎰   ference.

_ER (*Italian*). Thrice.

TER UNCA. The name formerly given to a demi-quaver.

TERZ (*German*). ⎱ The interval of a third.
TERZA (*Italian*). ⎰

TERZETTO (*Italian*). A short trio or piece for the or instruments.

TERZINA (*Italian*). A triplet.

TETRACHORD   A system of four sounds

THEILE. (*German plural*). Parts or capital divisions of the bar.

THÊME (*French*). A subject.

THEORBO. An ancient stringed instrument of the lute kind

THEORIE (*French*). Theory.

THEORICIEN (*French*). A theorist. One acquainted with the theory of music.

THIRTY-SECOND-NOTE. A demisemiquaver

THOROUGH BASS. The art of accompanying a figured bass on the piano or organ.*

TIBIA (*Latin*). The ancient name of wind instruments with holes, such as the flute.

TIERCE (*French*). The interval of a third. Also the name of an organ-stop tuned a major third higher than the Fifteenth.

TIERCE DE PICARDIE (*French*). A term applied to the concluding chord of a piece of music in a minor key, when its third is made major by an accidental sharp or natural.

TIMBALLES (*French*). The kettle-drums.

TIMBRE (*French*). The quality of sound produced by voice or instrument.

TIMBREL. An ancient Hebrew instrument like a tambourine.

TIMOROSO (*Italian*). With timidity and awe.

TIMPANI (*Italian plur.*). The kettle-drums.

TINTINNABULUM (*Latin*). A little bell.

TIRANNA. A Spanish national air.

TIRASSE (*French,* The pedals of an organ which act only upon the bass keys.

---

* See Hamilton's Catechism on Harmony and Thorough B

TIRA TUTTO (*Italian*). A pedal or draw-stop in an organ which, acting upon all the stops, at once enables the player to obtain the full power of the instrument.

TIRÉ (*French*). Drawn. This term is used in violin music to denote a *down bow.*

TOCCATA (*Italian*). A movement of difficult execution for a single instrument, generally the pianoforte.

TOCCATINA (*Italian*). A short toccata.

TON (*French*). A tone, or interval of a major second. Also the pitch of any note.

TON (*French*). The key; as, *le ton d'ut*, the key of C.

TONART (*German*). Mode.

TONAUSWEICHUNG (*German*). Modulation.

TONATILLAS (*Spanish*). National Spanish airs sung to a guitar accompaniment.

TONFÜHRUNG (*German*). Modulation.

TONIC. The key-note is so called by theorists.

TONIQUE (*French*). The tonic or key-note of a piece.

TONKUNST (*German*). The science of music.

TONLEITER (*German*). The scale.

TONSCHLUSS (*German*). A cadence.

TONS DE L'EGLISE (*French*) The Church modes or tones.

TONSETZER (*German*). A composer.

TONSTÜCK (*German*). A musical composition.

TONSTUFE (*German*). A degree of the stave.

TONWISSENSCHAFT (*German*). The science of music.

TOUCHES (*French*). The keys of the piano or organ.

TRACHEA (*Latin*). The windpipe.

TRADOTTO (*Italian*). Arranged, adapted.

TRAIT (*French*). A run or passage.

TRAITÉ (*French*). ⎫ A treatise either on the practice or
TRATTATO (*Italian*). ⎬ the theory of music.

TRANQUILLAMENTE (*Italian*).
TRANQUILEZZA, con (*Italian*). } Tranquilly, composedly.
TRANQUILLITÀ, con (*Italian*).
TRANQUILLO (*Italian*).

TRANSIENT MODULATION. That which continues but a short time.

TRANSPOSED. Removed into another key.

TRAVERSIÈRE (*French*). } The German flute.
TRAVERSO (*Italian*).

TRE (*Italian*). Three; as *à tre*, for three voices or instruments.

TREBLE. The acute part, that which in general contains the melody.

TREMENDO (*Italian*). With a tremendous expression, horribly.

TREMANDO (*Italian*). } Imply the reiteration of a
TREMOLANDO (*Italian*). note or chord with great rapidity, so as to produce a
TREMOLATE (*Italian*). tremulous kind of motion.
TREMOLO (*Italian*).

TRENISE (*French*). One of the movements of the quadrille.

TRIAD. A chord of three notes, a common chord.

TRIBRACH. A musical foot composed of three short notes.

TRICINIUM. A composition in three parts.

TRILLANDO (*Italian*). A succession of shakes on different notes.

TRILLE (*French*). }
TRILLER (*German*). } A shake.
TRILLO (*Italian*). }

TRILLERKETTE (*German*). A chain of shakes.

TRILLETTE (*French*). A short trill or shake.

TRINKLIED (*German*). A Bacchanalian or drinking song.

TRIO (*Italian*). A piece for three **voices or instruments**. This term also denotes a second movement to a waltz, march, minuet, &c. which always leads back to a repetition of the first or principal movement.

TRIOLET (*French*). A triplet.

TRIPLE CROCHE (*French*). A demisemiquaver.

TRIPLE COUNTERPOINT. Counterpoint in three parts, all of which are invertible.

TRIPLE TIMES. Such as have an *odd* number of parts in a bar.

TRIPLET. A group of three notes arising from the division of a note into three equal parts of the next inferior duration.

TRISAGION. A hymn in which the word HOLY is repeated, three times in succession.

TRITONE.
TRITONO (*Italian*). } A superfluous or augmented fourth.
TRITONUS *Latin*).

TROCHEE. A dissyllabic foot, composed of one long and one short syllable.

TROMBA (*Italian*). A trumpet.

——— DI BASSO (*Italian*). The bass trumpet.

——— MARINA (*Italian*). The trumpet marine, a species of monochord.

TROMBETTA (*Italian*). A small sized trumpet.

TROMBONE (*Italian*). A very powerful and rough-toned instrument of the trumpet kind, but much larger, and with a sliding tube.

TROMBONNE (*French*). The trombone.

TROMPETTE (*French*). The trumpet.

TROUP. A quick march.

TROPPO (*Italian*). Too much; as, non troppo allegro, not too quick.

TROMMEL (*German*). The great drum.

TROMP DE BEARN (*French*). The Jew's harp.

TROPPO CARICATA (*Italian*). Too greatly overburdened; as an air with too many or too heavy accompaniments. &c

TROUBADOUR (*French*). An itinerant bard, or musician-poet, in the times of chivalry.

TRUGSCHLUSS (*German*). An interrupted cadence.

TUONI ECCLESIASTICI (*Italian plu*). The ecclesiastical modes or tones.

TURCA, *alla* (*Italian*). In the Turkish style.

TUTTA FORZA (*Italian*). With the utmost vehemence, as loud as possible.

TUTTE CORDE (*Italian plur*). Upon all the strings. This term is sometimes met with in music for the piano, to imply that the pedal which shifts the movement must no longer be pressed down.

TUTTA (*Italian*).⎫ All, the whole: as, *tutto arco,* with the
TUTTO (*Italian*).⎭ whole length of the bow.

TUTTE (*Italian plural*).⎫ All. A term used to point out
TUTTI (*Italian plural*).⎭ those passages where all the voices or instruments, or both, are to be introduced.

TWELFTH. The name of an organ-stop tuned twelve notes above the diapasons. Also, an interval of twelve degrees.

TYROLIENNE (*French*). A dance peculiar to to the inhabitants of the Tyrol.

U.

ÜBERMÄSSIG (*German*). Augmented, superfluous in regard to intervals.

UBUNG (*German*). An exercise or study for any musical instrument.

UDITO (*Italian*). The sense of hearing.

UDITORE (*Italian*). An auditor, a hearer.

UGUALE (*Italian*).
UGUALMENTE (*Italian*). } Equally, all alike.

UMANA (*Italian*). Human: as. *voce umana*, the human voice.

UMKEHRUNG (*German*). Inversion, in speaking of choras.

UN (*Italian*).
UNA (*Italian*). } A ; as, *un poco*, a little.
UNO (*Italian*).

UNA CORDA (*Italian*). Implies that a passage is to be played upon only one string.

UNCA (*Latin*). The old name for a quaver.

UNEQUAL VOICES. Those compositions in which male and female voices are employed are said to be for *unequal voices*.

UNESSENTIAL NOTES. Those which form no part of the harmony.

UNGERADE TAKTART (*German*). Triple time.

UNHARMONISCHER QUERSTAND (*German*). A false relation.

UNISONI (*Italian plural*). This term implies that two. three, or more parts, are to play in unison with each other; or, if this be not practicable at least in octaves.

UNISONO (*Italian*). A unison.

UT. A monosyllable used by the French, to name and solfa the note C.

UT QUEANT LAXIS (*Latin*). The commencing words of the hymn to St. John the Baptist, from which hymn Guido is said to have taken the syllables, *ut, re, mi, fa, sol, la,* for his system of solmisation.

V

V. is used by the Italians as an abbreviation of the word Violin; as are VV. for Violini or Violins

VA (*Italian*). Go on: as, *va crescendo*, continue to increase in loudness.

VAGO (*Italian*). With a vague expression.

VALCE (*Italian*).⎱ A waltz; as, *Valse de l'oiseau*, a bird
VALSE (*French*). ⎰ waltz*.

VALSE A DEUX TEMS (*French*). A modern waltz, in which the dancers make two steps in each measure.

VARIAMENTO (*Italian*). In a varied and free style of execution.

VARIAZIONI (*Italian plural*). Variations upon an air or theme.

VARIÉ (*French*). Varied; as, *air varié*, an air with variations.

VALEUR (*French*). Duration or value of the notes.

VAUDEVILLE (*French*). A short interesting dramatic entertainment, interspersed with little airs.

VEEMENTE (*Italian*). ⎱ Vehemently, forcibly.
VEEMENZA, con (*Italian*). ⎰

VELATO (*Italian*). Veiled, indistinct.

VELLUTATO (*Italian*). Softly and smoothly.

VELOCE (*Italian*). ⎱ In a rapid time. This term is
VELOCITÀ, con (*Italian*).⎰ sometimes used to signify that a particular passage is to be played as quick as possible.

VELOCISSIMO (*Italian*). With extreme rapidity.

VENEZIANA, alla (*Italian*). In the Venetian style.

---

* See three very elegant Waltzes, under this title, by Chaulieu, published by Cocks an Co.

VERÄNDERUNGEN (*German plural*). Variations.

VERBINDUNG (*German*). Combination.

VERMINDERTE (*German*). Diminished, in speaking of intervals.

VERSE. A portion of an anthem or service intended to be performed by one singer to each part, and *not* in chorus like the rest.

VERSE ANTHEM. An anthem containing one or more verses.

VERSE SERVICE. A Service in which verses are introduced.

VERSETTE (*German*). Short movements for the organ, intended as preludes, interludes, or post-ludes to psalm-tunes, &c.

VERSETTO (*Italian*). A short or little verse.

VERSETZEN (*German*). To transpose.

VERSETZUNG-ZEICHEN (*German*). Marks of transposition: the *sharp*, the *flat*, and the *natural*.

VERSI SCIOLTI (*Italian*). Blank verse.

VERWANDT (*German*). Related, relative as to the keys.

VERWECHSLUNG (*German*). A change or mutation.

VERZIERUNG (*German*). Embellishment, variation.

VESPERÆ (*Latin*). Vespers or evening service in the Catholic Church.

VESPERS. The evening service in the Catholic Church.

VIBRANTE (*Italian*). A peculiar manner of touching the keys of the piano.

VIBRATISSIMO (*Italian*). The superlative of *vibrato*.

VIBRATE (*Italian*). } With a strong, vibrating quality of
VIBRATO (*Italian*). }   tone.

VIDO *Italian*). } Terms used in music for such stringed
VUIDE (*French*). } instruments as the violin, violoncello, &c. to signify that a particular note must be played on the open string.

VIELLE (*French*). The hurdy-gurdy.

VIERTELNOTE (*German*). A crotchet.

VIGOROSAMENTE (*Italian*) }
VIGOROSO (*Italian*). } Boldly, vigorously.

VILANELLE (*French*). }
VILLANELLA (*Italian*). } An old rustic dance accompanied with singing.

VIOLA (*Italian*). The tenor violin.

VIOL D'AMORE (*Italian*). }
VIOLE D'AMOUR (*French*. } An instrument with six strings, resembling the violin.

VIOL DA GAMBA (*Italian*). An instrument resembling the violoncello, but mounted with six strings.

VIOLENTEMENTE (*Italian*). }
VIOLENZA, con (*Italian*). } With violence.

VIOLINO (*Italian*). The violin.

VIOLINO PRINCIPALE (*Italian*). The first or principal violin part.

VIOLINSCHÜSSEL (*German*). }
VIOLINZEICHEN (*Germnn*). } The treble clef.

VIOLON (*French*). A violin.

VIOLONCELLE (*French*). }
VIOLONCELLO (*Italian*). } The bass violin.

VIOLONO (*Italian*). The double bass.

VIRGINAL. A keyed instrument much used during the reign of Elizabeth.

VIRTUOSO (*Italian*). One who greatly excels on some particular instrument.

VITAMENTE (*Italian*). }
VITE (*French*). } With quickness.
VITEMENT (*French*). }

VIVACE (*Italian*). }
VIVACEMENTE (*Italian*). } With briskness and animation,
VIVACITA, con (*Italian*). } vivaciously.
VIVAMENTE (*Italian*). }

VIVACISSIMO (*Italian*). With extreme vivacity.

VIVENTE (*Italian*).
VIVEZZA, con (*Italian*). } Animated, lively
VIVO (*Italian*).

VOCALIZE. To practise singing on the vowels, chiefly the Italian A.

VOCALIZZI (*Italian*). Vocal exercises to be sung on the vowels.

VOCE (*Italian*). The voice.

—————— DI CAMERA (*Italian*). A voice suited for private rather than for public singing.

—————— DI PETTO (*Italian*). The chest or natural voice.

—————— DI TESTA (*Italian*). The head voice, that is, the falsetto or feigned voice.

VOLANTE (*Italian*). In a light and rapid manner

VOLATA (*Italian*).
VOLATE (*French*).
VOLATINA (*Italian*). } A rapid succession of notes.
VOLATINE (*French*).

VOLKSLIED (*German*). A national song.

VOLL (*German*). Full; as, *mit volle Orgel*, full organ.

VOLLKOMMEN (*German*). Perfect.

VOLONTÉ (*French*). Will, pleasure; as, *à volonté*, at will.

VOLTA (*Italian*). Time of playing a movement; as, *prima volta*, the first time of playing; *seconda volta*, the second time, &c.

VOLTE (*Italian*). An obsolete dance resembling the Galliard, written in $\frac{3}{4}$ time.

VOLTI SUBITO (*Italian*). Turn over the page quickly.

VOLUBILITÀ, con (*Italian*). } With volubility and freedom
VOLUBILMENTE (*Italian*). } of performance.

VOLUNTARY. A piece for the organ, generally consisting of two or three movements, calculated to display the capabilities of the instrument and the skill of the player.

VON (*German*). *By;* often occurs in German titles.

VORAUSNAHME (*German*). Anticipation.

ORBEREITUNG (*German*). Preparation, a term used in harmony.

VORHALT (*German*). A suspension or retardation.

VORSCHLAG (*German*). An appoggiatura.

VORSPIELE (*German*). Preludes to psalm-tunes, &c.

VORZEICHNUNG (*German*). The signature.

VUIDE (*French*). Open: as, *corde vuide*, in violin music, indicates the open string.

W.

WALZER (*German*). A waltz.

WAYGHTES.⎫ Persons who, about Christmas, play psalm-
WAITS. ⎭ tunes, &c. in the streets, during the night.

WECHSELNOTEN (*German plural*). Irregular transient notes, appoggiaturas.

WEICHE (*German*). Minor in respect to keys and mode

WEITE HARMONIE (*German*). Dispersed harmony.

WESENTLICH (*German*). Essential.

WHOLE NOTE. A semibreve (◯).

WIEDERHOLUNG (*German*). Repetition.

WINDLADE (*German*). The wind-chest of an organ.

WIRBEL (*German*). A peg of a violin, tenor, &c.

Z.

ZAMPOGNA, *alla* (*Italian*). In the style of the bagpipe.

ZARGE (*German*). The sides of any musical instrument; such as the violin, tenor, violoncello, guitar, &c.

ZEITMASS (*German*). The time or degree of movement.

ZELO, con (*Italian*).
ZELOSAMENTE (*Italian*). } With zeal, enthusiastically.
ZELOSO (*Italian*).

ZERSTREUT (*German*). Dispersed.

ZINGARESA, alla (*Italian*). In the gipsy style.

ZINKE (*German*). A kind of rustic pipe, no longer used, cornet.

ZITHER (*German*). The guitar.

ZOPPO (*Italian*). In a limping manner. A style of melody in which a long note is always placed between two short notes.

ZUFÄLLIG (*German*). Accidental.

ZUFFOLO (*Italian*). A little flute or flageolet, chiefly used to teach birds to sing.

ZURÜCKHALTUNG (*German*). Retardation.

ZUSAMMENGESETZT (*German*). Compound, in speaking of times.

ZWISCHENSPEIL (*German*). An interlude, in organ-playing.

ZWISCHENRÄUME (*German*). The spaces between the lines of the stave.

ZWEISTIMMIG (*German*). For two voices or parts.

ZWEYFACHE INTERVALLEN (*German plural*). Compound intervals.

ZWEYKLANG (*German*). A chord of two sounds.

ABBREVIATIONS.

A

accel. .... Accellerando   Allo...... Allegro

Acc ..
Accom. } Accompagnamento

Alltto..... Allegretto

All 8va. ..All' ottava

Ad lib....Ad libitum   Al Seg....Al Segno

Ado......Adagio   Andno....Andantino

Affettc....Affettuoso   And'e.....Andante

Affreto....Affrettando   Arpo.....Arpeggio

A temp. ....A tempo

B

C. ....Basso Continuo.   Brill. ....Brillante

C

Calo. ....Calando   Clar. .....Clarinet

C.B......Contrabasso   Con Esp.. Con Espressione

Cello ....Violoncello   Cres.....Crescendo

D

D.C. ....Da Capo   Dim. ....Diminuendo

Decres. ..Decrescendo   Dol......Dolce

Dolciss............Dolcissimo

E

Energe...Energicamente   Espress.. Espressivo

F

F........Forte   Fl. ......Fiauto or Flanti

FF..........Fortissimo   Fz. ......Forzando

FFF   ..Very fortissimo

Fp. ......Forte, and then Piano; when applied to a single note
it marks a strong accent.

G

Grand°...Grandioso   Graz°....Grazioso

I

Introd..........Introduzione

L

Leg. ....Legato   L.H.........Left nand

M

Maest°..Maestoso   M.S.....Mano sinistra

Man^do ..Mancando   Men. ...Meno

Magg....Maggiore   Min.....Minore

M.D.....Mano dritta   Mod°. ..Moderato

M.F ....Mezzo forte.   Mus.Bac. Bachelor of Musk

M.M.....Maelzel's Metronome   Mus.Doc.Doctor of Music

M.P. ....Mezzo piano   M.V.....Mezza voce

O

Ob......Oboè   Op......Cpera

8^d. or 8va.Ottava   Org°.....Chgaro

     alta.....Ottava alta, an octave higher

     bassa ...Ottava bassa, an octave lower

      8va.....Con ottava, with octaves

P

......Piano
Ped.....Pedal
Perden...Perdendosí
PF......Piano and then forte
Pizz. ....Pizzicato

PP.....Pianissimo
1ma......Prima
1mo......Primo
PPP.....Very pianissimo
Prestmo...Prestissimo

R

Raddo.. . Raddolcendo
Rallen.
Rallo .. } Rallentando
Recit .. Recitativo
R.H.....Right hand

Rf.....
Rfz.... } Rinforzando
Rinf. ..
Ritard. ...Ritardando
Riteu.....Ritenutc

S

Scherz.....Scherzando
Seg......Segno
Sem.....Sempre
Sf.......Sforzando
Smorz ....Smorzando

Sost. .. } Sostenuto
Sosten..
Sym.....Symphony
2da......Seconda
2do......Secondo

Stacc..........Staccato

T

T.S.... Tasto Solo
Tem. . ..Tempo

Ten.....Tenuto
Tr. ......Trillo

U

Unis...........Unisoni

V

Var......Variation
Va. ......Viola
Vo. ......Violino

Vllo......Violoncello
V.S.....Volti subito
V V.. ....Violini

PHRASES WHICH OCCUR IN MODERN AUTHORS.

Andante ma non troppo e con tristezza. Not too slow, but with pathos.

Andantino sostenute e semplicemente, il canto un poco più forte. In a sustained and simple style, with the melody somewhat louder than the other notes.

Colla più gran forza e prestezza. As loud and as quick as possible.

Come 'l primo tempo. In the same degree of movement as at first.

Come tempo del tema. Same degree of movement as the theme.

Cantabile, ornamenti ad libitum, ma più tosto pochi e buoni. In a singing style, with embellishments at will, but few and well chosen.

Con abbandono ed espressione. With self-abandon and expression.

Con brio ed animato. Animated and brilliant.

Con 8va ad libitum. With octaves at pleasure.

Crescendo ed incalcando poco a poco Gradually augmenting the power and increasing the time

Crescendo poco a poco. Increasing the sound by degrees.

Crescendo e poi diminuendo. Increasing and then diminishing the sound.

Da capo senza repetizione e poi la coda. Begin again, but without any repetition of the strain, and then proceed to the coda

Dolce con gusto. Sweetly and tastefully.

Dolce e lusingando. In a delicate and insinuating style.

Dolce e piacevolmente espressivo. Soft and with pleasing expression

Dolce ma marcato. Delicately, but still sufficiently marked.

FF. principalmente il basso. Very loud, especially the bass.

Il terzo dite a tutte le notte di basso. The third finger on all the notes in the bass.

Istesso valore, ma un poco più lento. The same duration, but rather slower.

L' istesso tempo poi a poi di nuovo vivente. The same time, with gradually increasing animation.

Moderato assai con molto sentimento. A very moderate degree of movement, with much feeling.

Piano, sempre staccato e marcato il basso. Soft, with the bass always well marked and detached.

Poco a poco, più di fuoco. With gradually increasing animation and fire.

Poco a poco crescendo, decrescendo. Louder, softer, by degrees

Poi a poi tutte le corde. All the strings, one after another. An expression used in playing the grand pianoforte.

Segue subito senza cambiare il tempo. Proceed directly and without changing the time.

Segue senza interruzione. Go on without stopping.

Sempre piano e ritenuto. Always more and more soft, and falling off in the degree of movement.

Sempre più decrescendo e più rallentando. Gradually softer and slower.

Sempre più forte......all ff^{mo}. Louder and louder to the fortissimo.

Seconda volta molto crescendo. Much louder the second time or playing.

Sin' al fine. To the end.

Tenete sino alla fine del suono. Keep down the keys as long as the sound lasts.

CHARACTERS USED IN MUSIC.

§ 1. *Names of the Notes.**

In England and in Germany the notes are named after the seven letters, A, B, C, D, E, F, G.

The only difference is that the Germans apply the letter *B* to B flat only, and call our B natural, *H*.

In Italy and France the notes are named

la, si, do, re, mi, fa, sol,

corresponding to our A, B, C, D, E, F, G.

These notes may be natural, sharp, or flat, and occasionally even double sharp, or double flat.

Thus we have C natural, C sharp, C flat, and, at times, C double sharp and C double flat.

In France and Italy these notes would respectively be called *do naturelle, do dieze, do bemol, do double dieze, do double bemol, &c.*

The Germans add to the letter which is used to denominate the note, in its natural state, *is,* when it is to be made *sharp,* and *es,* when flat : thus, with them,

C sharp   ———   is called cis,
C flat   ——————   ces.
C double sharp ——— ciscis.
C double flat ——— cesces.

---

* For a full explanation of the modern system of notation, see Hamilton's Musical Grammar, published by R. Cocks and Co., price 4s.

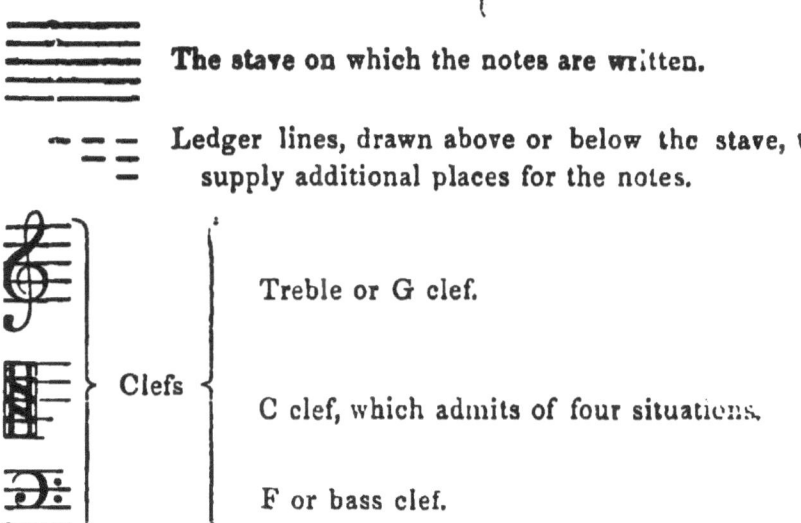

The stave on which the notes are written.

Ledger lines, drawn above or below the stave, to supply additional places for the notes.

Clefs
- Treble or G clef.
- C clef, which admits of four situations.
- F or bass clef.

§ 2. *Characters relating to the duration of the Notes, Rests, Dot, &c.*

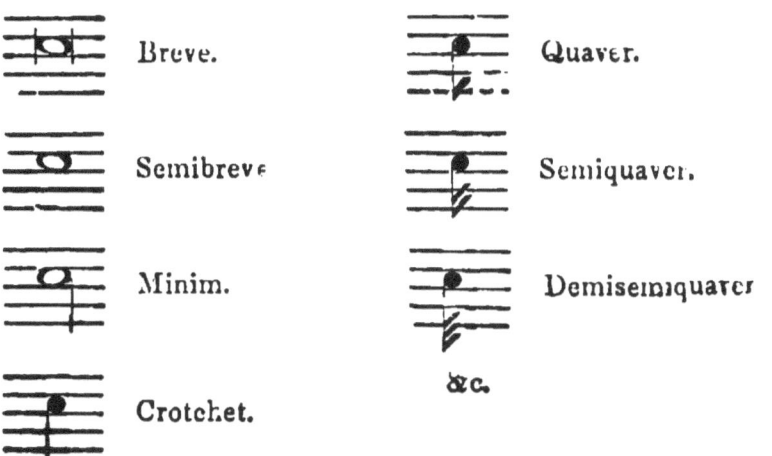

Breve.

Semibreve

Minim.

Crotchet.

Quaver.

Semiquaver.

Demisemiquaver

&c.

All the above notes may have one. two, or even three *dots* placed after them, to protract their duration.

Each note has a corresponding *rest*; as,

Breve rest, or two bars in any time.

Semibreve rest, or generally a single bar rest

Minim rest.

Crotchet rest.

Quaver rest.

Semiquaver rest.

Demisemiquaver rest.

&c.

Rests may be dotted, or doubly or triply dotted, like the notes which they represent.

Notes are sometimes divided into 3, 5, 7, 9, &c. equal parts, instead of 2, 4, or 8, as usual; in this case, the number of parts is expressed by a figure, and a curved line is drawn over it, thus: 3, 5, 7, 9, &c.

§ 3. *Marks of Transposition or Alteration of the pitch of the Natural Notes.*

♯   The sharp.

♭   The flat.

♮   The natural.

×   The double sharp.

♭♭   The double flat.

♮♯   Single sharp after a double sharp.

♮♭   Single flat after a double flat.

§4. *Table of Characters denoting the different Species of Time.*

⁝∣∣∣	Bar lines, dividing a movement into small equal portions of duration.	

C or ₵   Indicates two minims or four crotchets in each bar.

$\frac{2}{4}$ Indicates two crotchets in each bar.

$\frac{3}{2}$ ——— three minims ———

$\frac{3}{4}$ ——— three crotchets ———

$\frac{3}{8}$ ——— three quavers ———

$\frac{6}{4}$ ——— six crotchets ———

$\frac{6}{8}$ ——— six quavers ———

$\frac{12}{8}$ Indicates twelve quavers in each bar.

$\frac{12}{16}$ ——— twelve semiquavers ———

$\frac{9}{4}$ ——— nine crotchets ———

$\frac{9}{8}$ ——— nine quavers ———

$\frac{9}{16}$ ——— nine semiquavers ———

§5. *Other Characters affecting the Duration of the Notes.*

A *bind* or *tie*, which connects two or more notes of the same name into one longer note.

A *pause*, which lengthens at will the duration of a note or rest.

§6. *Characters indicating the various degrees of Loud and Soft.*

Indicates a *crescendo*, or gradual increase of tone.

Indicates a *decrescendo*, or gradual decrease.

Indicates first a *crescendo*, and then a *decrescendo*.

Indicates first a *decrescendo* and then a *crescendo*.

§ 7. *Marks of Accent and Expression.*

$\begin{cases} \overset{>}{} \\ V \\ \wedge \\ \vdots \\ \equiv \end{cases}$ Indicate a stress or marked accent on any single note or chord. The abbreviations *rf, sf fz, rfz, sfz, fp,* or even *f* over a single note, are also used for the same purpose.

❜ ❜ ❜ ❜ Dashes indicate notes struck very short, or staccato; that is, not held their full value.

. . . Dots, notes struck short, but not in so marked a way as the preceding.

⌒
• • • Curve and dots. Notes still less staccato. **This** is called the *mezzo staccato.*

⌒ Slur, or legato mark.

§ 8. *Graces.*

♩or ♪ Indicates the appoggiatura, where superior or inferior.

∿ Turn.

§ Inverted Turn.

♭
∿ Turn with the note above made flat.

∿
♯ Turn with the note below made sharp.

tr or *tr* ∿∿∿ A shake.

$\left. \begin{array}{c} \ggg \\ \text{or} \\ \sim\sim\sim \end{array} \right\}$ The vibration or close shake.

$\left(\text{or} \begin{cases} \\ \\ \end{cases} \right.$ Indicates that the chord before which it is placed must be sprinkled or arpeggined.

§ 9. *Characters used to separate a Movement into its component parts or strains, Marks of Repetition, &c.*

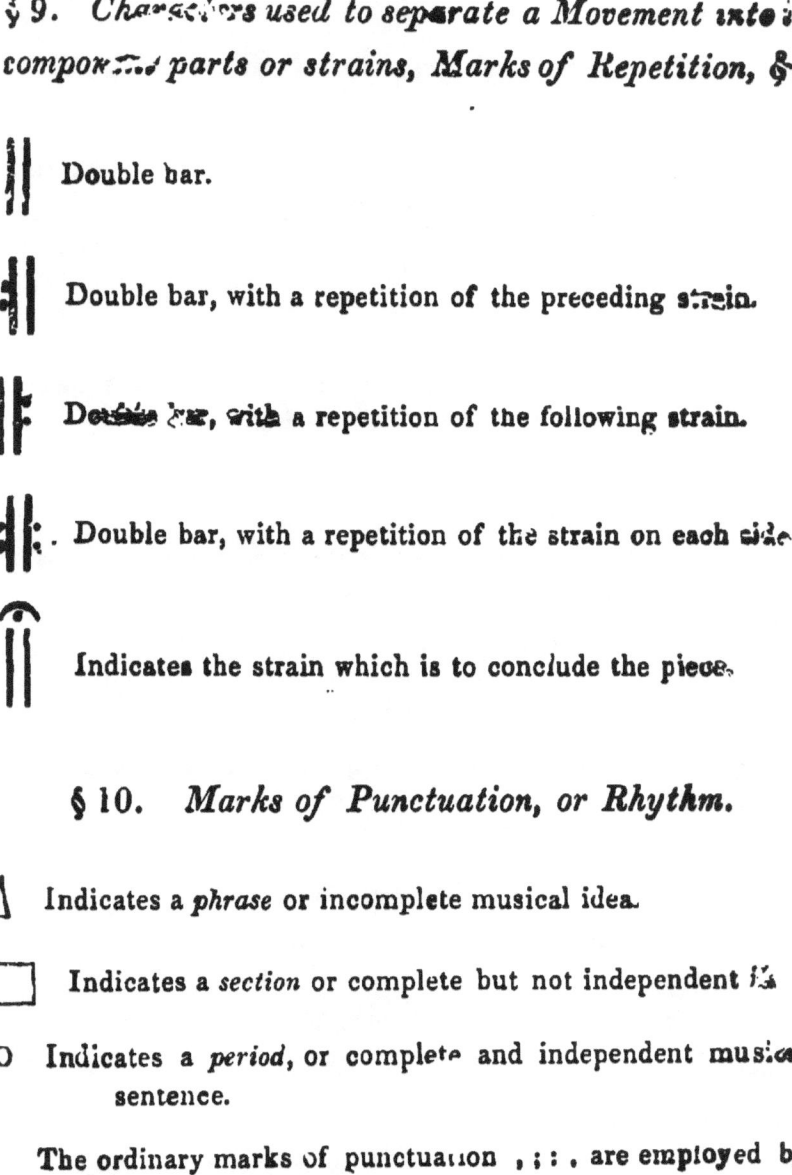

‖ Double bar.

╣‖ Double bar, with a repetition of the preceding strain.

‖╠ Double bar, with a repetition of the following strain.

╣‖╠ . Double bar, with a repetition of the strain on each side.

⌢‖ Indicates the strain which is to conclude the piece.

§ 10. *Marks of Punctuation, or Rhythm.*

△ Indicates a *phrase* or incomplete musical idea.

▢ Indicates a *section* or complete but not independent idea

O Indicates a *period*, or complete and independent musical sentence.

The ordinary marks of punctuation , ; : . are employed by some composers for a similar purpose.

§ 11.   *Miscellaneous Characters.*

{   A *brace*, used to connect two or more staves together in pianoforte, harp, and organ music, or in scores.

$\text{♩} = 120$
$\text{♪} = 80$

&c.

Mark the application of Maelzel's Metronome

⊕
♦
·♦
✳
Ped.

are met with in pianoforte music, to indicate the use of the pedals.

ɯ   The direct; it is placed upon the same line or space as the note which begins the next line.

are often met with in violin music, the former to indicate a *down*, and the latter an *up*, bow

§ 12.   *Marks of Abbreviation.*

Indicates that the long note must be repeated as often as it occurs in quavers or semiquavers.

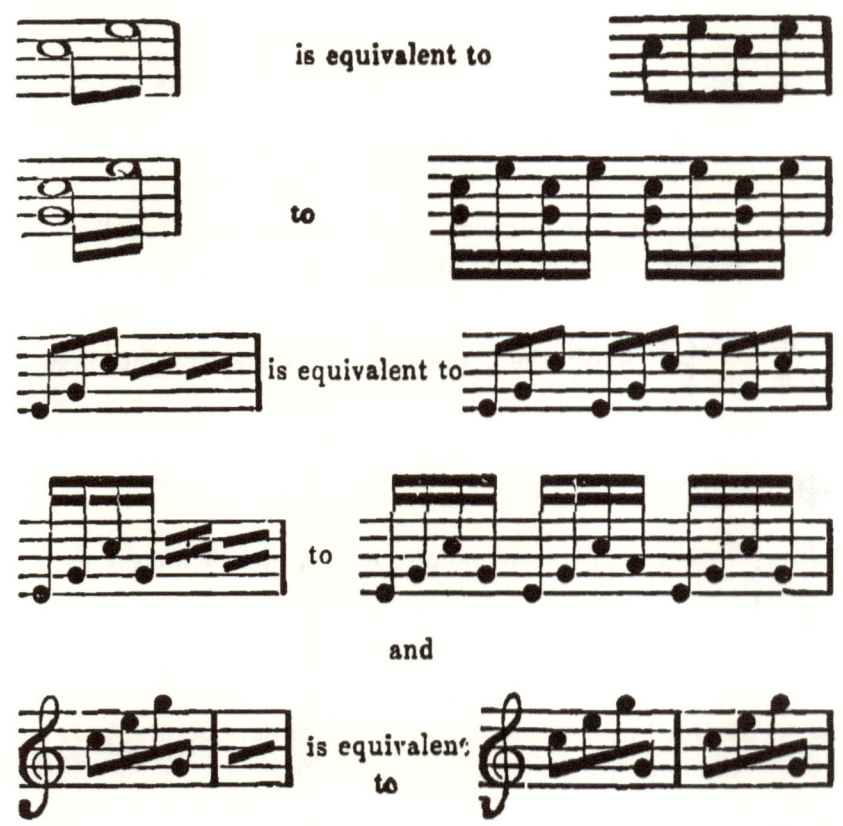

APPENDIX

to

HAMILTON'S DICTIONARY

CONSISTING OF

JOHN TINCTOR'S

"TERMINORUM MUSICÆ DIFFINITORIUM."

BIOGRAPHICAL NOTICE

OF

JOHN TINCTOR.

John Tinctor, Doctor of Laws and Canon of Nivelle, in Brabant, and previously First Chaplain and Cantor to Ferdinand of Arragon, King of Naples, was born at Nivelle about the year 1450. He wrote several excellent works on music, none of which, however, appear to have been printed, except the present "*Terminorum Musicæ Diffinitorium.*" This work ong remained unknown, until in the latter part of last century Forkel discovered a copy in the Library of the Duke of Gotha, of which he inserted an entire reprint in his "*Literatur der Musik,*" p. 204, and following; and Dr. Burney also discovered a copy in the Library of George III., which is now deposited in the British Museum.*

Although neither the date nor the place of publication is given in the work, Burney states, (but without adducing any authority,) that it was printed at Naples about the year 1474, and adds, that it "was doubtless not only the *first Musical Dictionary* that was ever compiled, but the *first book* that was *printed* on the subject of music in general." †

The following are the titles of the existing manuscript works by Tinctor, a brief account of some of which may be seen in Becker's "*Systematisch Chronologische Darstellung der musikalischen Literatur,*" p. 567 :—

"*Tractatus musices.*"—"*Explanatio manus.*"—"*De tonoum natura ac proprietate.*" — "*De notis ac pausis.*"—"*De*

---

* Forkel, Gerber, and Lichtenthal have incorrectly stated that Burney found the copy in the Royal Library at Paris. The pres mark of the copy in the British Museum is, *King's Lib*: 66. *e.* 121.

† *History of Music*, vol. ii. p 458 (in note).

D

regulis, valore, imperfectione et alteratione notarum." *—*" De arte contrapuncti."—" Proportionale musices."—" De origine musicæ."*†—*" Complexus effectuum musicæ."* ‡

Some of Tinctor's practical works are preserved, according to Baini, in the archives of the Papal Chapel.§ The precise time of his decease is unknown. La Borde says he was living in 1494,‖ and Walther, that he flourished in 1495.¶ A more recent writer, however, says he died about the year 1520.**

In the 23rd volume of the Leipsig *" Allgemeine Musika-ische Zeitung,"* p. 229, mention is made of Choron being about to publish a French translation of Tinctor's complete works, but wh .ther this was ever accomplished does not appear.

In order to render this little Dictionary useful to the musical antiquary, and the learned reader in general, it has been deemed desirable to add Tinctor's *" Terminorum Musicæ Diffinitorium,"* as an Appendix. It is therefore here reprinted from Forkel's work before-mentioned.

The original has been preferred to a translation, first, from its being more satisfactory for reference; and secondly, from the terms being mostly found in ancient Latin works, by the readers of which a translation will not be required. The general student, however, will find an explanation of such of the terms as are still used, in the Dictionary.

October, 1849.   J. B.

---

* See La Borde's *Essai sur la Musique* vol. iii. p. 370.
† See Gerber's *Neues Lexikon der Tonkunstler*, vol. iv., p. 360.
‡ See Becker's *Musikalische Literatur*, p. 567.
§ See Kandler—*Ueber das Leben und die Werke des Palestrina,* p. 234; also the original work of Baini,—*Memorio Storico-Critiche delle Vita e delle Opere di Palestrina,* vol. i. notes 226 and 431.
‖ *Essai sur la Musique,* vol. iii. p. 238.
¶ See Walther's *Musicalisches Lexicon,* p. 609.
** Schilling's *Lexicon der Tonkunst,* Art. *Tinctor.*

TERMINORUM MUSICÆ DIFFINITORIUM.

Ioannis Tinctoris: Ad illustrissimam Virginem et Domi-
nam D. Beatricem de Aragonia: Diffinitorium Musicæ
fœliciter incipit:

Prudentissimæ Virgini ac illustrissimæ dominæ D. Bea-
trici de Aragonia: Serenissimi principis divi Ferdinandi dei
gratia regis Siciliæ Hierusalem: et Hungariæ probissimæ
filiæ: Ioannes Tinctoris: eorum qui Musicam profitentur
insimus voluntariam ac perpetuam servitutem.   Moris est
cuiuslibet scientiæ præceptoribus inclita virgo: dum ingeni-
orum suorum exercitia litteris mandant: aut ea viris illustribus:
aut claris dirigere mulieribus.   Cujus profecto motivum arbi-
tror: Vel ut eorum opera majorem habeant auctoritatem: vel
ut ipsorum animos: qui multum illis prodesse possunt quod
proprium virtutis est, sibi concilient.   Ego autem enitens tuam
(non adulescentulorum more: sed stabilitate et constantia) bene-
volentiam captare: tibi semper et præ omnibus morem gerere
cupio.   Quod mihi profuturum haud modicum expecto: si
tibi ipsa persuadeas et plurimum debere: a quo plurimum dili-
geris.   Quamobrem artis liberalissimæ ac inter mathematicas
honestissimæ: videlicet divinæ musicæ studiosus: nunc a
substantia: nunc ab accidenti suos diffinire terminos uti.issi-
mum existimans quibus intellectis de ea acturi facilius et naturam ejus et suarum partium comprehendent.   Præsens opusculum quod rationabiliter diffinitorium musicæ dicetur: ad
honorem tuæ celsitudinis ædidi æditumque tibi mulierum

clarissimæ dirigendum censui. Confidens id pergratum for
tibi: quæ a poematibus oratoriis muneribus et aliis artibu
bonis in quibus quod pulcherrimum excellis prudentissimæ
secedens animi recreandi contemplatione ad hanc artem iocundissimam te confers non modo deductionem in omni suo genes
per alios more principum Persarum atque Medorum: sed etiam
per te ipsam assumens. Quo præstantissimum accedit nostræ
facultatis decus, si quam formosissimam quam illustrissimam
quam fontibus honesti habundantissimæ refectam: quam denique omnium dominarum et suæ ætatis et præteritorum et
futurorum temporum ab omni parte beatissimam cuncti prædicant ei studere dignatur. Atqui regia proles si in ipso opusculo aliquid imperfectum quod te quam perfectissimam audeo
dicere non deceat sui perspectissimi viderint oculi: parce
precor. Nam (ut perclare Virgilius cecinit) Non omnia possumus omnes. Unde quum diversis naturaliter gaudens non
unica arte contentus plurium cognitionem attingere sicut
etiam discretio novit indies animo ferventi pertendam. Non
mirum si in qualibet adeo perfectus non evadam: ut illos qui
singulariter in singulis artibus operam et curam efficacissime
ponunt: vincere possim. Tamen si in theorica musices par
iter et praxi omnes nostri temporis cantores excedam aut excedar ab aliquo; tuæ cæ   rumque in ipsa arte peritissimorum perspicientiæ discutiendum relinquo. Se ipsum etenim
(ut prudentibus placet) laudare vani est vituperare stulti.

Diffinitiones Terminorum Musicalium :
et primo per A. incipientium
Capitulum I.

A est clavis locorum are et utriusque alamire.

ACUTÆ CLAVES acutа loca et acutæ voces sunt illæ et illa: quæ in manu ab alamire inferiori inclusive et usque ad alamire superius exclusive continentur.

ALAMIRE est locus cujus clavis est a: et in qua tres voces. S. lami et re canuntur. Et ipsum est duplex acutum et superacutum.

ALAMIRE ACUTUM est linca cujus clavis etiam a. et ir qua tres voces. S. la mi et re cantantur. la per naturam ex loco cfaut. mi per b molle ex loco f faut gravi. et re per bdurum ex loco g sol re ut gravi.

A LA MIRE SUPERACUTUM est spacium cujus clavis etiam a. et in quo tres voces. la mi et re cantantur. la per naturam ex loco c sol faut. mi per bmolle ex loco f faut acuto et re per bdurum ex loco g sol re ut acuto.

ALTERATIO est proprii valoris alicujus notæ duplicatio

AMBITUS est toni debitus ascensus et descensus

APOTOME est major pars toni: quæ semitonium majus vu.- gariter dicitur.

A RE est spatium cujus clavis est a. et in quo unica vox. S re canitur per bdurum ex loco Γ ut

ARMONIA est amenitas qvedam ex convenient' son- causata.

ARSIS est vocum elevatio.

AUGMENTATIO est ad aliquam notam dimidiæ partis. sui valoris proprii additio.

Per B. Capitulum Secundum.

B est clavis locorum bmi et utriusque bfabmi. Et est duplex videlicet quadrum et rotundum.

B QUADRATUM est clavis locorum bmi et utriusque bfabmi : designans ibi per b quadrum mi canendum esse.

B ROTUNDUM est clavis utriusque bfabmi, designans ibi per bmolle fa canendum esse.

B DURUM est proprietas : per quam in omni loco cujus clavis etiam g : ut canitur. et ex illo ceteræ voces deducuntur.

BFABMI est locus cujus una clavis est b. rotundum-altera b quadrum-et in quo duæ voces. S. fa et mi canuntur. Et est duplex. S. acutum et superacutum.

BFABMI ACUTUM est spacium cujus una clavis etiam b rotundum altera b quadrum et in quo duæ voces. S. fa et mi canuntur fa per bmolle: ex loco ffaut gravi et mi per bdurum ex loco gsolreut gravi.

BFABMI SUPERACUTUM est linea : cujus una clavis etiam b. rotundum altera b quadrum. Et in qua duæ voces S. fa et mi canuntur. fa per bmolle ex loco ffaut. et mi per bdurum ex loco g sol re ut acuto.

BMI est linea cujus clavis b quadrum etiam in qua mi canitur per bdurum ex loco Γ ut.

BREVIS est nota in tempore perfecto valoris trium semibrevium. Et in imperfecto duarum.

Per C. Capitulum Tercium.

C est clavis locorum cfaut. csolfaut. et csolfa.

CANON est regula voluntatem compositoris sub obscuritate quadam ostendens.

CANTILENA est cantus parvus : cui verba cujuslibet materiæ sed frequentius amatoriæ supponuntur.

CANTOR est qui cantum voce modulatur.

CANTUS est multitudo ex unisonis constituta : qui aut simplex aut compositus est.

CANTUS SIMPLEX est ille qui sine ulla relatione simpliciter constituitur et hic est planus aut figuratus.

CANTUS SIMPLEX PLANUS est qui simplicibus notis incerti valoris simpliciter est constitutus. cujusmodi est gregorianus.

CANTUS SIMPLEX FIGURATUS est qui figuris notarum certi valoris simpliciter efficitur.

CANTUS COMPOSITUS est ille qui per relationum notarum unius partis ad alteram multipliciter est æditus : qui refacta vulgariter appellatur.

CANTUS PER MEDIUM est ille in quo duæ notæ sicut per proportionem duplam uni commensurantur.

CANTUS UT JACET dicitur. qui plane sine ulla diminutione canitur.

CFAUT est spacium cujus clavis est c. et in quo duæ voces S. fa et ut caruntur. fa per bdurum ex loco Γ ut. et ut per naturum : ex loco proprio.

CIRCULUS est signum quantitatis temporalis : qui aut perfectus aut imperfectus est.

CIRCULUS PERFECTUS est signum temporis perfecti.

CIRCULUS IMPERFECTUS est signum temporis imperfecti : qui ab aliquibus semicirculus dicitur.

CLAVIS est signum loci lineæ vel spacii.

CLAUSULA est cujuslibet partis cantus particula in fine cujus vel quies generalis vel perfectio revertitur.

COLOR est identitas particularum in una et eadem parte cantus existentium quoad formam et valorem notarum et pausarum suarum.

COMA est illud in quo tonus superat duo semitonia minora.

COMPOSITOR est alicujus novi cautus æditor.

CONCORDANTIA est fonorum diversorum mixtura dulciter auribus conveniens. Et hæc aut perfecta aut imperfecta est.

CONCORDANTIA PERFECTA est: quæ continue pluries ascendendo vel descendendo fieri non potest. ut unisonus diapenthe sub et supra quantum vis diapason.

CONCORDANTIA IMPERFECTA est quæ continue pluries ascendendo vel descendendo fieri potest. ut dytonus semidytonus diapenthe cum tono et diapenthe cum semitonio sub et supra quantum vis diapason.

CONJUNCTA est dum fit de tono regulari semitonium irregulare aut de semitonio regulari tonus irregularis. Vel sic.

CONJUNCTA est appositio b rotundi aut b quadri in loco irregulari.

CONJUNCTIO est unius vocis post aliam continua junctio.

CONTRAPUNCTUS est cantus per positionem unius vocis contra aliam punctuatim effectus. Et hic duplex. S. simplex et diminutus

CONTRAPUNCTUS SIMPLEX est: dum nota vocis quæ contra aliam ponitur est ejusdem valoris cum illa.

CONTRAPUNCTUS DIMINUTUS est: dum plures notæ contra unam per proportionem æqualitatis aut inæqualitatis ponuntur. qui a quibusdam floridus nominatur.

CONTRA TENOR est pars illa cantus compositi. quæ principaliter contra tenorem facta inferior est supremo altior autem aut æqualis aut etiam ipso tenore inferior.

CONTRA TENORISTA est ille qui contra tenorem canit.

CSOLFA est spacium cujus clavis est c. et in quo duæ ꞇꞁꞇꞁꞇꞁ
S. sol et fa canuntur: sol per bmolle ex loco ffaut acuto
et fa per bdurum ex loco gsolreut acuto.

ꞇSOLFAUT est linea cujus clavis est c. et in qua tres voces.
S. sol fa et ut canuntur. sol per bmolle ex loco ffaut gravi. fa
per bdurum ex loco gsolreut gravi. et ut per naturam ex
loco proprio.

Per D. Cap. Quartum.

D. est clavis locorum dsolre. dlasolre et dlasol.

DEDUCTIO est vocum de uno loco ad alium per aliquam pro-
prietatem ordinatam ductio.

DIAPASON equivocum est ad tria. nam concordantiam
coniunctionem et proportionem significat. Pro primo sic
diffinitur.

DIAPASON est concordantia ex mixtura duarum vocum
abinvicem perfecto diapenthe et diatesseron aut imperfecto
diapenthe et tritono distantium effecta. Pro secundo sic.

DIAPASON est conjunctio ex distantia perfecti diapenthe et
diatesseron. aut imperfecti diapenthe et tritono constituta.
Pro tercio sic.

DIAPASON est proportio qua major numerus ad minorem
relatus illum in se bis continet precise. ut duo ad unum. iiii.
et ad. ii. Et hic adverte quam quotiescunque diapason per se
invenitur: de perfecto intelligitur. Est. n. triplex. s. perfectum, imperfectum: et superfluum.

DIAPASON PERFECTUM est illud quod constat ex
quinque tonis et duobus semitonis. ut a mi de bmi usque ad
mi de bfabmi acuto.

DIAPASON IMPERFECTUM est illud quod constat ex
quatuor tonis et tribus semitonis .ut. a mi de bmi · usque ad
fa de bfabmi acuto.

DIAPASON SUPERFLUUM est illud quod constat ex sex tonis et uno semitonio minori. ut a fa de ufabmi acuto: usque ad mi de bfabmi superacuto. et ista duo ultima discordantia sunt.

DIAPENTHE tria significat. s. concordantiam. conjunctionem et proportionem. Pro primo autem significato sic diffinitur.

DIAPENTHE est concordantia ex mixtura duarum vocum abinvicem diatesseron et tono. aut tritono et semitonio distantium effecta. Pro secundo sic.

DIAPENTHE est conjunctio ex distantia diatessaron et toni. aut tritoni et semitonii constituta. Et pro tercio sic.

DIAPENTHE est proportio qua major numerus ad minorem relatus illum in se totum et insuper ejus alteram partem aliquotam continet. ut sunt tria ad duo. sex ad quatuor. Nunc autem notandum est triplex esse diapenthe. s. perfectum, imperfectum et superfluum.

DIAPENTHE PERFECTUM est illud: quod constat ex tribus tonis et uno semitonio. ut a mi de elami gravi usque ad mi de bfabmi acuto.

DIAPENTHE IMPERFECTUM est illud quod' constat ex duobus tonis et duobus semitoniis. ut a mi de elami gravi usque ad fa de bfabmi acuto.

DIAPENTHE SUPERFLUUM est illud quod constat ex tribus tonis et uno semitonio majori. ut si fa in elami acuto fingatur: et contra hoc mi in bfabmi superacuto ponatur, Et hæc duo ultima diapenthe sunt discordantia. ubicunque vero diapenthe sine aliqua adjunctione ponitur: de perfecto intelligitur.

DIAPENTHE cum semitonio equivocatur ad duo. Nam et concordantiam et conjunctionem designat. Unde pro primo significato sic diffinitur.

DIAPENTHE cum semitonio est concordantia ex mixtura duarum vocum diapenthe et semitonio abinvicem distantium effecta. Et pro secundo sic.

DIAPENTHE CUM SEMITONIO est conjunctio ex distantia diapenthe et semitonii constituta.

DIAPENTHE CUM TONO duo significat. scilicet. concordantiam: et conjunctionem. Hinc pro primo significato sic diffinitur.

DIAPENTHE CUM TONO est concordantia ex mixtura duarum vocum diapenthe et tono distantium effecta. Et ita pro secundo sic.

DIAPENTHE CUM TONO est conjunctio ex distantia diapenthe et toni constituta.

DIAPENTHE CUM SEMIDITONO pro duplici significato accipitur. scilicet pro discordantia et conjunctione. Vnde pro primo sic diffiniendum est.

DIAPENTHE CUM SEMIDITONO est discordantia ex mixtura duarum vocum abinvicem diapenthe et semiditono distantium effecta. Et pro secundo sic.

DIAPENTHE CUM SEMIDITONO est coniunctio ex distantia diapenthe et semiditoni constituta.

DIAPENTHE CUM DITONO equivocum est ad duo: ad discordantiam. S. et coniunctionem. Hinc pro primo significato sic diffinitur.

DIAPENTHE CUM DITONO est discordantia ex mixtura duarum vocum ab invicem diapenthe et ditono distantium effecta. Et pro secundo sic.

DIAPENTHE CUM DITONO est conjunctio ex distantia diapenthe et ditoni constituta.

DIAPHONIA idem est quod discordantia.

DIATESSARON etiam tria habet significata S. concordantiam, conjunctionem et proportionem Pro primo significato sic diffinitur.

DIATESSARON est concordantia secundum quid ex mixtura duarum vocum ab invicem tono et semiditono vel econtra distantium effecta. Pro secundo sic.

DIATESSARON est conjunctio ex distantia duorum tonorum cum semitono præposito aut postposito vel intermisso constituta. Et pro tercio sic.

DIATESSARON est proportio qua major numerus ad minorem relatus: illum in se totum continet et ejus insuper terciam partem aliquodam. ut iiii. ad iii. et **VIII.** ad **VI.**

DIASTEMA idem est quod coma.

DIESIS est una pars toni in quinque divisi.

DIMINUTIO est alicujus grossi cantus in minutum redactio.

DISCANTUS est cantus ex diversis vocibus et notis certi valoris æditus.

DISCORDANTIA est diversorum sonorum mixtura naturaliter aures offendens.

DITONUS æquivocum est ad duo. nam concordantiam et coniunctionem designat. Vnde primo significato sic diffinitur.

DITONUS est concordia ex mixtura duarum vocum ab invicem duobus tonis distantium effecta. Et pro secundo sic diffinitur.

DITONUS est conjunctio ex duarum tonorum distantia constituta.

DIVISIO est unius aut plurium notarum ab illa seu ab illis cum qua vel cum quibus regulariter est annumeranda vel sunt annumerandæ separatio.

DLASOL est linea cuius clavis est d. et in qua duæ voces. S la et sol canuntur. la per bmolle ex loco ffaut acuto. et so per bdurum: ex loco gsolreut acuto.

DLASOLRE est spacium cuius clavis est d. et in quo tres voces. S. la sol et re canuntur. la per bmolle ex loco ffaut gravi. sol per bdurum ex loco gsolreut gravi. et re per ﹖ ﹖﹖ram ex loco csolfaut.

DSOLRE est linea cujus clavis est d. et in qua duæ voces. s. sol et re canuntur. sol per bdurum ex loco Γ ut. et re per naturam ex loco cfaut.

DUO est cantus duarum tantum partium relatione ad invicem compositus.

DUPLA idem est quod diapason. Vnde secundum tria ejus significata instar diapason diffinitur.

DUPLA SEXQUIALTERA est proportio qua maior numerus ad minorem relatus : illum in se bis continet : et ejus insuper alteram partem aliquotam. ut. V. ad. ii. et X. ad. iiii.

DUPLA SUPERBIPARTIENS est proportio qua maior numerus ad minorem relatus : illum in se bis continet, et insuper eius duas partes aliquotas unam facientes aliquantam. ut. VIII. ad tria. et XII. ad V.

Per E. Capitulum V.

E est clavis utriusque elami. et ela.

ELA est spacium . cuius clavis est e. et in quo unica vox. 8. la canitur per bdurum ex loco gsolreut acuto.

ELAMI est locus, cuius clavis est e. et in quo duæ voces. s. la et mi canuntur. Et est duplex. grave et acutum.

ELAMI GRAVE est spacium : cuius clavis est e. et in quo duæ voces. s. la et mi canuntur. la per bdurum ex loco Γ ut. et mi per naturam ex loco cfaut.

ELAMI ACUTUM est linea : cuius clavis est e : et in qua duæ voces. s. la et mi canuntur. la per bdurum. ex loco gsolreut gravi et mi per naturam ex loco csolfaut.

EMIOLIA idem est quod diapenthe. unde sicut diapenthe secundum tria ejus significata eam diffinies.

EPYGDOUS tria significat. scilicet discordantiam conjunctionem et proportionem. Pro primo eius significato sic diffinitur.

EPYGDOUS est discordantia ex mixtura duarum vocum tono ab invicem distantium effecta. pro secundo sic.

EPYGDOUS est conjunctio ex distantia toni constituta. et pre tercio sic.

EPYGDOUS est proportio qua major numerus ad minorem relatus: illum in se totum continet et eius insuper octavam partem, ut sunt. IX. ad VIII. et XVIII. ad XVI.

EPYTRITUS idem est quod diatessaron. Hinc secundum tria ejus significata: ut diatessaron diffinietur.

EUFONIA idem est quod armonia.

EXTRACTIO est unius partis cantus ex aliquibus notis alterius confectio.

Per F. Capitulum VI.

F. est clavis utriusque ffaut.

FA est quarta vox distans a tercia semitonio: et a quinta tono.

FA SOL est mutatio quæ fit in csolfaut. et in csolfa: ad descendendum de bduro in bmolle.

FA UT est mutatio quæ fit in cfaut et in csolfaut. ad ascendendum a bduro in naturam et in utroque ffaut ad ascendendum a natura in bmolle.

FFAUT est locus cujus clavis est f. et in quo duæ voces. s fa et ut canuntur. et est duplex. scilicet. grave et acutum.

FFAUT GRAVE est linea cuius clavis est f. et in qua duæ voces. s. fa et ut canuntur. fa per naturam ex loco cfaut. et ut per molle ex loco proprio.

FFAUT ACUTUM est spacium cuius clavis est f. et in quo duæ voces. s. fa et ut canuntur. fa per naturam ex loco csolfaut, et ut per bmolle ex loco proprio.

FICTA MUSICA est cantus propter regularem manus traditionem æditus.

FUGA est idemtitas partium cantus quo ad valorem, nomen formam: et interdum quoad locum notarum et pausarum suarum.

Per G. Cap. VII

G est clavis ut.

G est clavis utriusque gsolreut.

Γ UT est linea cuius clavis est Γ. et in qua unica vox. s. ut per bdurum ex loco proprio canitur.

GRAVES CLAVES gravia loca et graves voces sunt illæ et illa quæ in manu ab are inclusive usque ad alamire exclu‐ sive continentur

GRAVISSIMUS LOCUS est Γ ut. gravissima clavis et gra‐ vissima vox illius.

GSOLREUT est locus: cuius clavis est g. et in quo tres voces. s. sol re et ut canuntur. Quod quidem duplex est. s. grave et acutum.

GSOLREUT ACUTUM est linea. cuius clavis est g. et in qua tres voces. sc. sol re et ut canuntur: sol per naturam ex loco csolfaut. re per bmolle ex loco ffaut acuto. et ut per bdurum: ex loco gsolreut acuto.

GSOLREUT GRAVE est spacium: cujus clavis est g. et in quo tres voces: s. sol re et ut canuntur. sol per naturam ex loco cfaut. re per bmolle ex loco ffaut gravi. et ut per bdurum ex loco proprio.

Per H. Capitul. VIII.

HYMNUS est laus dei cum cantico.

HYMNISTA est ille qui hymnos canit.

Per I. Cap. IX.

IMPERFECTIO est tertiæ partis valoris totius notæ an‐ partim ipsius abstractio.

INSTRUMENTUM est corpus naturaliter aut artificialiter soni causativum.

INTONATIO est debita cantus inchoatio.

IUBILUS est cantus cum excellenti quadam leticia pronunciatus.

Per L. Cap. X.

LA est sexta et ultima vox: tono distans a quinta.

LAMI est mutatio quæ fit in utroque elami: ad ascendendum a bduro in naturam. et in utroque alamire a natura in bmolle.

LARE est mutatio quæ fit in utroque alamire: ad ascendendum a natura in bdurum: et in dlasolre ad ascendendum a bmolli in naturam.

LA SOL est mutatio quæ fit in dlasolre et in dlasol. ad ascendendum de bmolli in bdurum.

LIGATURA est unius notæ ad aliam iunctura.

LIMA est minor pars toni: quam alii semitonium minus appellant.

LINEA est locus tractu quodam designatus: quam alii regulam dicunt.

LOCUS est vocum situs.

LONGA est nota in modo minori perfecto valoris trium brevium. in imperfecto duorum.

Per M. Cap. XI.

MANUS est brevis et utilis doctrina. ostendens compendiose deductiones vocum musicæ.

MAXIMA est nota in modo maiori perfecto valoris trium longarum. et in imperfecto duarum.

MELODIA idem est quod armonia.

MELOS idem est quod armonia.

MELUM idem est quod cantus.

MENSURA est adæquatio vocum quantum ad pronunciationem.

MI est tercia vox: tono distans a secunda et semitonio a quarta.

MILA est mutatio quæ fit in utroque elami: ad descendendum de natura in bdurum. et in utroque alamire: ad descendendum de bmolli in naturam.

MINIMA est nota valoris individui.

MIRE est mutatio quæ fit in utroque alamire ad ascen. pendum a bmolli in bdurum.

MISSA est cantus magnus: cui verba Kyrie. Et in terra. Patrem. Sanctus: et Agnus. Et interdum cæteræ partes a pluribus cauendæ supponuntur. quæ ab aliis officium dicitur.

MODUS est quantitas cantus ex certis longis maximam: aut brevibus longam respicientibus constituta. Est igitur duplex scilicet major et minor.

MODUS MAJOR est quantitas cantus ex certis longis maximam respicientibus constituta: qui subdividitur. Nam alius est perfectus alius imperfectus.

MODUS PERFECTUS est dum tres longæ pro una maxima numerantur.

MODUS vero **MAJOR IMPERFECTUS** est: dum duæ tantum longæ pro una maxima numerantur.

MODUS MINOR est quantitas cantus ex certis brevibus longam respicientibus constituta. Qui etiam subdividitur. Nam alius est modus minor perfectus: alius imperfectus.

MODUS MINOR PERFECTUS est dum tres breves pro una numerantur.

MODUS MINOR IMPERFECTUS est dum duæ tantummodo breves pro una longa numerantur.

MOTETUM est cantus mediocris: cui verba cujusvis materiæ sed frequentius divinæ supponuntur.

MULTIPLEX proportionum genus est: quo maior numerus ad minorem relatus: illum in se plusquam semel continet. ut duo ad unum, tria ad unum, quatuor ad unum.

MULTIPLEX SUPERPARTICULARE proportionum genus est: quo maior numerus ad minorem relatus: illum in se totum plus quam semel continet: et ejus insuper unam partem aliquotam. ut V. ad ii. VII ad III. novem ad quatuor.

MULTIPLEX SUPERPARTIENS proportionum genus est: quo maior numerus ad minorem relatus: illum in se plusquam semel continet. et eius insuper aliquas partes aliquotas facientes tamen unam partem aliquantam ut sunt octo ad tria. XI. ad IIII. et XIV. ad V.

MUSICA est modulandi peritia cantu sonoque consistens. Et hæc triplex est. scilicet. **Armonica. Organica.** ae etiam Rithmica.

MUSICA ARMONICA est illa: quæ per vocem practicatur humanam.

MUSICA ORGANICA: est illa quæ fit in instrumentis flatu sonum causantibus.

MUSICA RITHMICA est illa quæ fit per instrumenta tactu sonum reddentia.

MUSICUS est qui perpensa ratione beneficio speculationis canendi officium assumit. Hinc differentiam inter musicum et cantorem quidam sub tali metrorum serie posuit. **Versus.**

> Muisicorum et cantorum magna est differentia.
> Illi sciunt ipsi dicunt quæ componit musica.
> Et qui dicit quod non sapit reputatur bestia.

MUTATIO est unius vocis in aliam variatio.

Per N. Cap. XII.

NATURA est proprietas per quam in omni loco cuius clavis est c. ut cantatur. et ex illo cæteræ

NEOMA est cantus fini verborum sine verbis annexus.
NOTA est signum vocis certi vel incerti valoris.

Per O. Cap. XIII.

OCTAVA idem est quod diapason aut dupla coniunctio et
concordantia. Vnde secundum hæc duo significata: eam
ut diapason diffinies.

DEFICIUM idem est quod missa secundum hispalos.

Per P. Cap. XIV.

PAUSA est taciturnitatis signum: secundum quantitatem
notæ cui appropriatur fiendæ.

PERFECTIO equivocum est ad duo. Nam notæ in sua
perfectione permanentiam : et totius cantus aut particularem
ipsius conclusionem designat. Vnde pro primo significato
sic diffinitur.

PERFECTIO est, dum æqualiter notæ maneat perfectæ
ostensic. Et pro secundo sic.

PERFECTIO est totius cantus aut particularum ipsius
perfectionis cognitio.

PROLATIO est quantitas cantus ex certis minimis semi-
brevem respicientibus constituta. Quæ quidem duplex est.
scilicet major et minor.

PROLATIO MAJOR est: dum in aliquo cantu tres minimæ
pro una semibrevi numerantur.

PROLATIO MINOR est: dum in aliquo cantu duæ cantum
minimæ pro una semibrevi numerantur.

PRONUNCIATIO est venusta vocis emissio.

PROPORTIO est duorum numerorum ad invicem habitudo.
Et hæc est duplex. s. equalitatis et inequalitatis.

PROPORTIO EQUALITATIS est quæ ex equalibus numeris
conficitur ut duo ad duo. iii. ad iii. et iiii. ad iiii.

PROPORTIO INEQUALITATIS est quæ ex inequalibus numeris fit. ut duo ad unum. iii. ad duo. et cætera. Et hic adverte: quæ in præsenti diffinitorio genera proportionum cum quibusdam speciebus suis diffinivi. Si vero plures habere cupias: in nostro proportionali musices invenies illas.

PROPRIETAS est propria quædam vocum producendarum qualitas.

PUNCTUS est signum augmentationis aut divisionis aut perfectionis. Et hoc si alicui notæ adjungatur. Si vero in circulo aut semicirculo a parte dextra aperto ponatur: significat quæ prolatio maior est. Et si in semicirculo ab inferiori parte aperto ponatur: moram generaliter fiendam in illa nota supra quam constituitur designat. Qui punctus organi vulgariter dicitur.

Per Q.   Capitulum XV.

QUADRUPLA est proportio: qua maior numerus ad minorem relatus: illum in se quater precise continet. ut IIII. ad unum. et octo ad duo.

QUADRUPLA SEXQUIALTERA est proportio: qua maior numerus ad minorem relatus: illum in se quater continet. et eius insuper partem aliquotam. ut IX. ad. ii. et XVIII. ad. IV.

QUADRUPLA SUPERBIPARTIENS est proportio: qua major numerus ad minorem relatus: illum in se quater continet: et eius insuper duas partes aliquotas: unam facientes aliquantam. ut. XIIII. ad tria. et. XXII. ad quinque.

QUANTITAS est secundum quam quantus sit cantus intelligitur

QUARTA idem est quod diatesseron coniunctio et concordantia. Hinc secundum hæc duo significata sicut diatesseron diffinitur.

QUINTA idem est quod diapenthe concordantiam et coniunctionem importans. Igitur sicut diapenthe quo ad hæc duo significata diffinietur.

Per R. Cap. XVI.

RE est secunda vox tono distans a prima totidem vero a tercia.

REDUCTIO est unius aut plurium notarum cum maioribus quas imperficiunt aut cum sociis annumeratio.

REGULA idem est quod linea.

RE LA est mutatio quæ fit in utroque alamire ad descendendum de bduro in naturam. et in dlasolre: ad descendendum de natura in bmolle.

ᴚE MI est mutatio: quæ fit in utroque alamire ad ascendendum de bquadro in bmolle.

RES FACTA idem est quod cantus compositus.

RE SOL est mutatio quæ fit in dsolre et in dlasolre: et in utroque gsoireut ad descendendum de bmolii in naturam.

RESUMTIO est cantus finiti ut pertinet replicatio.

RE UT est mutatio quæ fit in utroque gsolreut. ad ascendendum a bmolli in bduruin.

Per S. Cap. XVII.

SECUNDA equivocatur ad duo. s. ad discordantiam et coniunctionem. Vnde pro primo significato sic diffinitur.

SECUNDA est discordantia ex mixtura duarum vocum. tono vel semitonio ab invicem distantium effecta. Et pro secundo sic.

SECUNDA est coniunctio ex distantia unius toni vel semitonii constituta.

SEMIBREVIS est nota in prolatione maiori valoris trium minimarum et in minori duarum.

SEMITONIUM duo significat. sc. discordantiam et coniunctionem. Hinc pro primo significato sic dif·

SEMITONIUM est discordantia ex mixtura duarum ocum; duabus aut tribus diesibus ab invicem distantium effecta. Et pro secundo sic.

SEMITONIUM est conjunctio ex distantia duarum aut trium diesium constituta. Et i a collige duplex esse semitonium sc. majus et minus.

SEMITONIUM MAJUS est illud: quod ex tribus diesibus constat. ut de mi in bfabmi : usque ad fa in eodem loco. quo a pluribus apothome seu semitonium diatonicum appellatur.

SEMITONIUM MINUS est illud: quod ex duabus diesibus tantummodo constat. ut de mi in alamire usque ad fa in bfabmi. quod a Platone lima: ab aliis semitonium Enarmonicum appellatur. Est et aliud semitonium quod Cromaticum dicitur. Fit autem dum canendo aliqua vox ad pulcritudinem pronunciationis sustinetur. Quotiescunque vero semitonium per se scriptum invenitur. aut dicitur: minus esse intelligitur.

SEMIDITONUS est equivocum ad duo. s. ad concordantiam et conjunctionem. Vnde pro primo significato sic diffinitur.

SEMIDITONUS est concordantia ex mixtura duarum vocum tono et semitonio ab invicem distantium effecta. Et pro secundo sic.

SEMIDITONUS est coniunctio ex distantia unius toni et semitonii constituta.

SEMICIRCULUS idem est quod circulus imperfectus.

SEPTIMA PERFECTA idem est quod diapenthe cum ditono.

SEPTIMA IMPERFECTA idem est quod diapenthe cum semiditono.

SEXQUIALTERA idem est quod diapenthe aut emiolia proportio. Vnde secundum hoc significatum sicut illa diffinitur.

SEXQUITERCIA idem est quod diatesseron aut epitritus proportio. Hinc instar ipsorum quoad id significatum diffinienda est.

SEXQUIQUARTA est proportio qua major numerus ad minorem relatus: illum in se totum continet et insuper eius quartam partem aliquotam. ut. V. ad. IIII. et X. ad XVIII.

SEXTA PERFECTA idem est quod diapenthe cum tono.

SEXTA IMPERFECTA idem est quod diapenthe cum semitonio.

SINCOPA est alicuius notæ interposita maiore per partes divisio.

SOL est quinta vox tono distans a quarta totidemque ab ultima.

SOL FA est mutatio quæ fit in csolfaut et in csolfa. ad descendendum de bmolli in bdurum.

SOLFISATIO est cantando vocum per sua nomina expressio.

SOL LA est mutatio quæ fit in dlasolre et in dlasol: a descendendum de bduro in bmolle.

SOL RE est mutatio quæ fit in dsolre et in dlasolre: ad descendendum de bduro in naturam. et in utroque gsolreut: ad ascendendum a natura in bmolle.

SOL UT est mutatio quæ fit in utroque gsolreut: ad ascendendum a natura in bdurum. et in csolfaut: ad ascendendum de bmolli in naturam.

SONITOR est qui instrumento artificiali: sive organico sive rithmico musicam exercet.

SONUS est quicquid proprie et per se ab auditu percipitur.

SPACIUM est locus supra vel infra lineam relictus.

STEMA est dimiduum comatis.

SUBDUPLA est proportio qua minor numerus ad majorem relatus: in illo bis precise continetur, ut unam ad duo.

SUBMULTIPLEX proportionum genus est: quo minor numerus ad maiorem relatus in illo multipliciter precise continetur ut unum ad duo. et. I. ad. III.

UPERACUTA LOCA et superacutæ voces suut illæ et illa: quæ ab alamire superiori usque ad ela inclusive in manu continentur.

SUPERBIPARTIENS est proportio: qua maior numerus ad minorem relatus: illum in se totum continet et insuper duas eius partes aliquotas unam facientes aliquantam. ut. V. ad. III.

SUPERPARTICULARE proportionum genus est: quo maior numerus ad minorem relatus: illum in se totum continet: et ejus aliquam partem. aliquotam. ut. III. ad. II. et ISII. ad. III.

SUPERPARTIENS proportionum genus est: quo major numerus ad minorem relatus: illum in se totum continet. et ejus insuper aliquas partes aliquotas: unam facientes aliquantam ut quinque ad tria. et. VII. ad. V.

SUPPOSITIO est aliquorum corporum ut voces loco notarum signiticient introductio.

SUPREMUM est illa pars cantus compositi: quæ altitudine cæteras excedit.

Per T. Capit. XVIII.

T. est littera quæ per se ad aliquam partem cantus posita: tenorem institutione significat. quæ quidem si prima sit mei cognominis: quod Tinctoris est: mihi non dedecori venit quum et nomen domini ineffabile Tetagramaton ab ea sumat exordium.

TALEA est indemtitas particularum in una et eadem parte cantus existentium quoad nomen locum et valorem notarum et pausarum suarum

TEMPUS est quantitas cantus ex certis semibrevibus brevem respicientibus constituta. Quod quidem duplex est. sc. perfectum et imperfectum.

TEMPUS PERFECTUM est dum in aliquo cantu tres semibreves pro una brevi numerantur.

TEMPUS IMPERFECTUM est dum in aliquo cantu duæ semibreves tantum pro una brevi numerantur.

TENOR est cujusque cantus compositi fundamentum relationis.

TENORISTA est ille qui tenorem canit.

TERCIA PERFECTA idem est quod ditonus.

TERTIA IMPERFECTA idem est quod semiditonus.

TESIES est vocum depositio.

TONUS equivocum est ad quatuor. Nam significat coniunctionem, discordantiam, intonationem et tropum. Hinc pro primo significato sic diffinitur.

TONUS est coniunctio ex distantia quinque diesum constituta. Et pro secundo sic.

TONUS est concordantia ex mixtura duarum vocum quinque diesibus ab inviciem distantium effecta. Et pro tercio sic.

TONUS est cantus intonatio. Et pro quarto sic.

TONUS est tropus per quem omnis cantus debite componitur. Hujus autem significati octo sunt toni.

TONUS PRIMUS est ille: qui ex primis speciebus diapenthe et diatessaron formatus: potest a suo fine diapason ascendere ac ditonum descendere. qui ab antiquis auctenticus protus appellatus est.

TONUS SECUNDUS est ille: qui ex primis speciebus diapenthe et diatessaron formatus: potest a suo fine diapenthe cum ditono aut cum semiditono ascendere: qui plagalis aut subiugalis aut collateralis auctentici. Prothi ab antiquis dicitur.

TONUS TERCIUS est ille: qui ex secundis speciebus diapenthe et diatessaron formatus: potest a suo fine diapason ascendere. ac ditonum vel semiditonum descendere. qui ab antiquis auctenticus deuterus est appellatus.

TONUS QUARTUS est ille: qui ex secundis speciebus dia penthe ac diatessaron formatus: potest a suo fine diapenthe cum ditono aut semiditono ascendere: ac diatessaron descendere. qui plagalis aut subjugalis aut collateralis auctentici deuteri ab antiquis dicitur.

TONUS QUINTUS est ille qui dicitur ex tercia aut quarta specie diapenthe et tercia specie diatessaron formatus. et potest a fine suo diapason ascendere. ac ditonum vel semiditonum descendere. qui ab antiquis auctenticus tritus dicitur.

TONUS SEXTUS est ille: qui ex tercia aut quarta specie diapenthe et tercia specie diatessaron formatus: potest a suo fine diapenthe cum ditono aut semiditono ascendere. ac diatesseron descendere: qui plagalis aut subiugalis aut collateralis auctentici. Triti a musicis antiquis appellatus est.

TONUS SEPTIMUS est: qui ex quarta specie diapenthe et prima specie diatessaron formatus: potest a suo fine diapason ascendere. ac ditonum vel semiditonum descendere: qui ab auctoribus antiquis auctenticus Tetrardus est appellatus:

TONUS OCTAVUS est ille: qui ex quarta specie diapenthe et prima specie diatessaron formatus: potest a suo fine diapenthe cum ditono aut cum semiditono ascendere. ac diatessaron descendere: qui plagalis aut subiugalis aut collateralis auctentici tetrardi ab antiquis dicitur.

Istorum autem tonorum: alii sunt regulares: alii irregulares: alii mixti. alii commixti. alii perfecti: alii imperfecti. alii plusquamperfecti.

TONUS REGULARIS est qui in loco sibi regulariter determinato finitur.

TONUS IRREGULARIS est: qui in alio loco quam in illo qui sibi regulariter est determinatus finem accipit.

    Locus autem regularis primi et secundi toni est dsolre.

    Locus regularis tercii et quarti toni est elami grave.

    Locus regular⁚   est ffꝫut.

Locus vero regularis septimi et octavi est gsolreut grave.
Cætera vero loca sunt irregularia.

ꓔONUS MIXTUS est: qui si auctenticus fuerit descensum
sui plagalis. Si vero plagalis : ascensuḿ sui auctentici
attingit.

ꓔONUS COMMIXTUS est ille: qui si auctenticus fuerit:
cum alio quam cum plagali suo. Si vero plagalis cum alio
quam cum suo auctentico miscetur.

TONUS PERFECTUS est qui perfecte suum implet ambitum.

TONUS IMPERFECTUS est cuius ambitus non est perfectus.

TONUS PLUSQUAMPERFECTUS est qui ultra suum
ambitum si auctenticus fuerit: ascendit. Si vero plagalis:
descendit.

TRIPLA est proportio: qua major numerus ad minorem relatus :
illum in se ter precise continet ut tria ad. I. et. VI. ad duo.

TRIPLUM antiqui posuerunt partem illam compositi cantus
quæ superiori magis appropinquabat.

TRITONUS duo significat. s. discordantiam et coniunctionem
Vnde pro primo significato sic diffinitur.

TRITONUS est discordantia ex mixtura duarum vocum
tribus tonis ab invicem distantium effecta. Et pro secundo
sic.

TRITONUS est conjunctio ex distantia trium tonorum constituta.

Per V. Capitulum XVIIII.

VNISONUS duo habet significata. scilicet. solum sonum et
concordantiam. Hinc pro primo significato sic diffinitur.

VNISONUS est elementum musicæ. Namque ex unisonis
cantus componitur omnis. Et tamen dicitur unisonus
quasi unis sonus. Pro secundo sic diffinitur.

VNISONUS est concordantia ex mixtura duarum vocum in uno et eodem loco positarum effecta. quem dicunt fontem et originem omnium concordantiarum. Et tunc dicitur unisonus: quasi una id est simul sonans.

VOX est sonus naturaliter aut artificialiter prolatus.

UT est prima vox tono distans a secunda.

UT FA est mutatio quæ fit in cfaut et in csolfaut ad descendendum de natura in bdurum. et in utroque fiaut: ad descendendum de bmoili in naturam.

UT RE est mutatio quæ fit utroque gsolreut ad descendendum a bduro in bmolle.

VT SOL est mutatio quæ fit in utroque gsolreut ad descendendum de bduro in naturam. et in csolfaut ad descendendum de natura in bmolle.

Ioannis Tinctoris ad Divam Beatricem de Arragonia Peroratio.

Hoc opusculum dei gratia solutum tibi gloriosissima Diva Beatrix tuus offert Ioannes Tinctoris. Quod ut benigne suscipias: auctorique faveas humilime praecatur. Qui non solum id: sed siqua alia anima corporis ac fortunae bona: si superorum dono collata sint: omnia tuo submittit imperio. Deum amplius exorans: ut talem qualem te fecit caeterarum scilicet Dominarum perfectissimam perpetuo servare tuerique dignetur. *Amen.*

PIANOFORTE COMPOSITIONS

BY

W. VINCENT WALLACE.

All Sheet Music at half the marked price.

Music for the Pianoforte by W. Vincent Wallace.—"Mr. Wallace's compositions have, from their distinguished and elegant character, attained a wondrous popularity, surpassing in their attractive qualities the works of all living composers for the Pianoforte. His adaptations of the Scotch and Irish melodies are beyond all praise; his mode of treating these beautiful airs is as striking and original as it is sweet and charming. They are never heard without exciting fresh admiration; and we have no doubt every pianoforte-player will feel that the possession of the whole series of these gems is a matter of necessity. We are able to state that the Messrs. Robert Cocks and Co. are appointed publishers of his Pianoforte Works for Great Britain and its Dependencies. The House of William Hall and Son, of New York, continue to be his sole publishers for the United States."—*Observer, Aug. 20th.*

" Mr. Wallace was a musician of the very first order, and his name will ever perhaps stand most prominently out in connection with his Pianoforte Music."—*Edinburgh Evening Courant, Oct.* 4, 1863.

" The lamented demise of Mr. Vincent Wallace has caused quite a demand for his productions, especially those of recent date."—*Brighton Gazette.*

SELECTION OF

Recent and Favourite Romances, &c.

Twilight. Romance....................	3	0
Forget me not. Romance	3	0
Croyez-moi. Romance.............................	3	0
La Plainte du Berger. Idylle	3	0
Graziella. Nocturne.............................	3	0
The Wild Rose. Rondo polacca........................	3	0

" The two beautiful romances—' Forget me not' and ' Twilight' . . . ' Croyez-moi' is another example of this captivating kind of composition."—*Brighton Examiner*.

" The death of Mr. Vincent Wallace will add to the interest always felt in whatever emanated from his pen. The above three romances are good specimens of his manner in this kind of composition, and are admirably suited for studies in expression and delicate accuracy of fingering."—*Orchestra, Oct.* 21.

THE WILD ROSE.—"A sort of lovely lesson, full of grand chords and sweet runs."—*Leeds Times*.

GRAZIELLA, LA PLAINTE DU BERGER, FORGET ME NOT. — " The author of *Maritana* and *Lurline* deservedly holds a place in the first rank of our vocal composers. But it is not so generally known that he is a pianist *de la première force*, and a most accomplished writer for that instrument. The three pieces are fine specimens of his talents in this way. They show a thorough knowledge of the genius and power of the instrument, which enables him to produce the greatest amount of effect at the smallest cost of mechanical difficulty. We find in them the brilliancy of Thalberg and the graceful melody of Mozart, while their execution is not beyond the reach of the generality of good performers."—*The Press*.

ELEGANT

FANTASIAS AND DRAWING-ROOM PIECES.

. . . . . " Those pieces that the art world now acknowledge to be first-rate, and, I may say with justice, are world-renowned." —H. J. St. Leger (*Orchestra, Dec.* 23).

The Oarsman's March	3	0
La belle Danseuse	4	0
Valse sentimentale	3	0
Swiss Melody	3	0
Gentle Spring	3	0
The Wild Rose. Rondo Polacca	2	6
Air de Ballet	3	0
The Moss Rose. Rondo alla Polacca	3	0
The Wedding Waltz	4	0
Victoire. Mazurka	3	0
La Fleur de Pologne. Mazurka	3	0
Chorus of Dervishes from Beethoven's " Ruins of Athens "	3	0
The Chimes of the New Palace at Westminster. Impromptu	4	0
A te Divina Immagine	2	6
Somebody, and O for ane and twenty, Tam. Impromptu	3	0
Gondellied	3	0
March of the Volunteer Rifles	3	0
The Shepherd's Roundelay	4	0
Andante, with variations (dedicated to Mrs. Anderson, Pianiste to the Queen)	4	0
Croyez-moi. Romance	3	0
La Plainte du Berger. Idylle	3	0
Souvenir des Indes orientales. Mélodie	3	0
Com' è gentil. Serenade from Don Pasquale, transcribed	3	0
Impromptu de Concert sur Robin Adair, composed expressly for, dedicated to, and performed by, Madame Arabella Goddard	4	0

FANTASIAS, &c.— *Continued.*   *s.*

Beethoven s celebrated Romance for the Violin, Op. 56	3
Beethoven's celebrated 2nd Romance for the Violin, trans.	3
Polka rüsse	2
Graziella. Nocturne	3
Styrienne, pour Piano	3
Galop brillant de Salon.........	3
Souvenir d'Idlewild. Esquisse	3
Grand Triumphal March, dedicated to the three Regts. of Guards	3
Souvenir d'Espagne, El nuevo Jaleo de Jeres	2
L'Absence. Romance	3
Le retour. Polka brillante	3
Fairy March	2
Twilight. Romance.........	3
Paganini's Andante Amoroso, transcribed	2
Mazurka Etude	3
Nocturne (dedicated to Mdlle. Gabriel).........	3
Grande Mazurke guerrière (ded. to the Empress Eugénie)	3
Nocturne (dedicated to Mrs. Horace Twiss)	3
Forget me not. Romance	3
The Surprise. Andante from Haydn's 3rd Symphony.	3
The Rosebud Polka, *beautifully illustrated in colours*.....	2
Il Sostenuto. Etude de Salon.........	3
Woodland Murmurs. Nocturne.........	2
Le Rêve. Romance	3
Marche militaire	3
Evening Star (Schottische)	2
Pretty Mary Waltz	2
The Anna Waltz	2
L'Hirondelle Waltz	2
La Gondola, Souvenir de Venise, Nocturne	3
Rondoletto Scherzo	2
La Donna è mobile (Ballad. Verdi's Rigoletto), trans....	2
Bella Figlia dell' Amore (Quatuor, Rigoletto), trans.....	2

Melodies Transcribed and Varied.

"Besides the creation of new music, Mr. Wallace has undertaken the delightful task—delightful to those in whose musical souls are treasured the old melodies descending like rivulets of fresh water out of the caves of time—of adapting them to the instrument of our day. . . . . This is the task—no, not *task*—the delightful recreation of Vincent Wallace—one in whom music is an inherent portion of nature, an attribute of the soul. What a heritage! What a destiny! His sphere is harmony and joy, and a lasting life even on earth. He mounts, he soars, he sings; he gives tune to his fellow mortals, and they sing. He forms for himself an abiding place in the palace, the hall, the city, the cottage, the human heart; in the manliest breast of heroism, in the fairest bosom of love. And when his own mortal part lies low in earth, the voice of his soul is still heard in palace, in hall, in city, in cottage, mingling in the echoes of those who sang a thousand years before; he and they to be heard still singing through new generations, on, and on, and on."—*Weekly News.*

FAVOURITE SCOTCH MELODIES, TRANSCRIBED.

"In his treatment of our national melodies, Mr. Wallace has been exceedingly happy—the variations being at once elegant, in keeping, and effective."—*Aberdeen Herald, May 29.*

	s.	d.
When ye gang awa', Jamie. Air known as Huntingtower	3	0
Oh! Nanny, and He's o'er the hills............................	3	0
Maggie Lauder	3	0
The weary pund o' tow, There's nae luck about the house	3	0
My love is like the red, red rose, and Come o'er the stream, Charlie	3	0

SCOTCH MELODIES, &c.—*Continued.*

	s.	*d.*
Roy's Wife, and We're a' noddin', Fantasia on............	3	0
Kinloch of Kinloch, and I'm o'er young to marry yet ...	3	0
The gloomy night is gathering fast, and The lass o' Gowrie	3	0
Auld Robin Gray, and The Boatie rows	3	0
Bonnie Dundee, My Nanny, O ! and My ain kind dearie	3	0
John Anderson my jo, and Thou hast left me ever, Jamie	3	0
Charlie is my darling, and The Campbells are coming, Fantasia on.................................	3	0
Scots wha hae, Fantasia on	3	0
Roslin Castle, and A Highland lad my love was born ...	3	0
Ye banks and braes (*see Duets*)	3	0
The yellow-haired laddie	3	0
Kelvin Grove, varied................................	3	0
Comin' through the rye	3	0
Auld lang syne, and The Highland laddie.................	3	0
Donald, and Duncan Gray, Fantasia on	3	0
The keel row (*see Duets*)	3	0
Jock o' Hazeldean................................	3	0
Logie o' Buchan................................	3	0
The Blue Bells of Scotland (*see Duets*)	3	0
Wandering Willie, and My love she's but a lassie yet ...	3	0
Highland Mary	3	0
Annie Laurie	2	6
Robin Adair, Impromptu sur	3	0
Corn riggs are bonnie	3	0

FAVOURITE IRISH MELODIES, TRANSCRIBED.

The Meeting of the Waters, and Eveleen's bower........	3	0
The Minstrel Boy, and Rory O'More	3	0
Flwo on, thou shining river, and Nora Creina	3	0
Kate Kearney, and Tow, row, row	8	0

IRISH MELODIES, &c.—*Continued.*

	s.	*d.*
My lodging is on the cold ground	3	0
Go where glory waits thee, and Love's young dream	3	0
Coolun, Garryowen, and St. Patrick's Day	3	0
The Soldier's Greeting	3	0
The last rose of summer (*see Duets*)	3	0
The harp that once through Tara's halls, and Fly not yet	3	0
The Bard's Legacy	3	0
O ! leave me to my sorrow	3	0
The Song of our Native Land, varied for piano	4	0

FAVOURITE ENGLISH AND OTHER MELODIES.

	s.	*d.*
La Luvisella, Favourite Neapolitan Melody	3	0
Recollections of Switzerland. Melody	3	0
Star of the evening, and Willie, we have missed you	3	0
Come where my love lies dreaming, transcribed	3	0
Good news from home	3	0
Russian air, known as " Those evening bells "	3	0
Rose, softly blooming (L. Spohr)	3	0
Home, sweet home (Sicilian air)	3	0
Schöne Minka, and the Russian National Hymn	3	0
Cease your funning, and the Lass of Richmond Hill	3	0
Réverie on The Banks of Allan Water	3	0
The Old Hundredth	4	0
Fading away. Ballad (Anne Fricker)	3	0
The Vesper Hymn	3	0
The mountain daisy. Song (G. Linley)	3	0
Alpine melody (*see Duets*)	2	0
I know that my Redeemer liveth (Handel's Messiah)	3	0
With verdure clad (Haydn's Creation)	3	0
German melody, varied	3	0

The Holy Family.

Book I. (*The Favourite Book.*) Piano Solo, 6s.

ADMIRED SACRED MELODIES
BY
THE MOST CELEBRATED COMPOSERS,
ARRANGED FOR THE PIANOFORTE AS SOLOS AND DUETS,
With ad. lib. Accompt. for Flute, Violin, and Violoncello

WILLIAM HUTCHINS CALLCOTT,
WITH AN EXQUISITELY BEAUTIFUL FRONTISPIECE, AFTER RAPHAEL, PRINTED IN OIL COLOURS BY BAXTER.

CONTENTS:

No.
1. HANDEL—"He was despised and rejected." from the Oratorio "Messiah.'
2. HUMMEL—"Blessed is he." from the celebrated Service in B flat.
3. MARCELLO—"There is a river the stream whereof," from a Psalm.
4. ROSSINI—"Now abideth Faith, Hope, and Charity, these three."
5. HAYDN—"I am the bright and Morning Star," from the Oratorio of "The Creation."
6. MENDELSSOHN—"As the hart desireth the water brook."
7. MOZART—"Glory to God in the highest." from the celebrated 2nd Service

THE SAME AS DUETS:

THE HOLY FAMILY—Arranged for four hands on one Pianoforte, by W. H. Callcott, 6s.
Accompaniment ad lib. for Flute, 1s.—Violin, 1s.—Violoncello, 1s.

R. BERT COCKS & Co. *have the satisfaction to announce that the above named elegant work—the most popular selection of Sacred Pianoforte Music that ever appeared—is now added to their Catalogue, they having, at a heavy outlay, acquired the Copyright at the Sale of Messrs Jullien's publications.*

"Messrs. ROBERT COCKS & Co.'s enterprise is already well known and has been universally acknowledged. It has often been our pleasing duty to call public attention to some musical novelty, possessing not only much intrinsic merit of its own, but displaying in the strongest possible light that spirit of enterprise which is their well known characteristic. We have to record another instance of it. They have lately purchased the valuable copyright—unquestionably one of the most valuable copyrights in the trade—of the above collection of sacred melodies from M Jullien, at a very large cost, and they now present the public with several choice selections from the great masters, arranged by Mr. CALLCOTT, who has performed his task with that skill and taste which the public are naturally led to expect at his hands. Public appreciation must be bestowed on a work which not only deserves but commands it."—*Vide Court Circular* Dec. 26, 1857.

No. 3.
MUSIC PORTFOLIOS.

No.

1. Music Folio with cloth back and corners, and papered board sides ..
2. Music Folio, with cloth back and corners, and papered board sides, superior quality, gilt extra .. ..
3. Music Folio, leather back and cloth board sides, gilt .. ..
4. Music Folio, superior, gilt extra .. ..
   "A very useful and serviceable folio."
5. Music Folio, gilt extra, with flaps to protect the edges of the music .. ..
6. Music Folio, with flaps, very superior, gilt extra .. ..
   "An excellent, elegant, and very durable folio."

SPRING BACK FOLIOS.

7. Music Folio, with spring back to secure the Music, whole cloth, gilt .. ..
8. Music Folio, with spring back to secure the Music, superior, gilt .. ..
9. A spring back Folio, suitable for "Musical Times." .. ..

PORTABLE FOLIOS.

10. A new and most portable Folio, specially adapted for carrying several pieces of Music without breaking them. The Music is folded once in the centre and secured with an elastic cord. It may be carried in the hand, under the arm, or in the pocket, leather, gilt ... .
11. Ditto .. Ditto, with flaps, gilt extra .. .. ..
12. Ditto .. Ditto, real Morocco .. .. ..
13. Ditto .. Ditto, very superior finish, with lock and key ..

MUSIC ROLLERS.

14. Good Black American Cloth .. ..
15. Best Black American Cloth, with superior strong coloured binding .. ..
16. Roller and Folio combined, in best American cloth .. ..
17. Best Roan leather, lined with cloth, and gilt border, extra ..
18. Best Morocco, gilt extra .. ..
   "A most serviceable roller, and the most durable."

MUSIC BOXES.

19. Box for holding Music, patent lid, gilt extra
20. Ditto, with lock and key .. ..

LONDON: ROBERT COCKS & CO., NEW BURLINGTON STREET, W.,
BY SPECIAL APPOINTMENT,
Music Publishers to Her Most Gracious Majesty Queen Victoria
and H.R.H. the Prince of Wales.

www.ingramcontent.com/pod-product-compliance
Lightning Source LLC
Chambersburg PA
CBHW030556040726
47497CB00008B/2744